PUFFIN BOOKS

Editor: Kaye Webb

MAGIC IN MY POCKET

The stories in this volume are drawn from seventeen of Alison Uttley's books, and include two – *The Easter Egg* and *Christmas is Coming* – from her first, THE COUNTRY CHILD, that unforgettable tale of childhood on a hill-country farm. Another – *Sledging* – comes from a later book of memories, COUNTRY HOARD. The rest are tales of imagination, most of them owing much to those keenly observant years when the ways of country things were so deeply absorbed and indelibly recorded. For this author everything has life; the wind calls, animals talk, the trees tell their secrets. She can truly say, 'There is magic in my pocket.'

Judith Brook has provided the decorations, catching enchantingly the lightness of the author's touch with both fact and fancy.

A selection of books by Alison Uttley

FOR CHILDREN

Sam Pig goes to Market
Sam Pig and Sally
Sam Pig in Trouble
Yours Ever, Sam Pig
The Spice-woman's Basket
The Weather Cock
The Cobbler's Shop
John Barleycorn
Nine Starlight Tales
Little Grey Rabbit Books
Little Brown Mouse Books

FOR ADULTS

The Farm on the Hill
Ambush of Young Days
The Country Child
Country Things
Carts and Candlesticks
Here's a New Day
A Traveller in Time
Buckinghamshire

Magic in My Pocket

A SELECTION OF TALES BY

ALISON UTTLEY

WITH DECORATIONS BY

JUDITH BROOK

Penguin Books

in association with Faber & Faber

Penguin Books Ltd, Harmondsworth, Middlesex, England
Penguin Books Inc., 7110 Ambassador Road, Baltimore, Maryland 21207, U.S.A.
Penguin Books Australia Ltd, Ringwood, Victoria, Australia

—

This selection of tales, which were first
published by Faber & Faber, first issued in
Puffin Books 1957
Reprinted 1961, 1964, 1965, 1968, 1969, 1971 (twice), 1972

—

—

Made and printed in Great Britain
by Cox & Wyman Ltd,
London, Reading and Fakenham
Set in Monotype Garamond

Contents

Tim Rabbit

THE wind howled and the rain poured down in torrents. A young rabbit hurried along with his eyes half shut and his head bent as he forced his way against the gale. He tore his trousers on a bramble and left a piece of his coat on a gorse-bush. He bumped his nose and scratched his chin, but he didn't stop to rub himself. He hurried and scurried towards the snug little house on the common where his mother was making bread.

At last he saw the open door, he smelled the warm smell of baking, and in he rushed without wiping his feet on the little brown doormat.

'What's the matter, Tim?' asked Mrs Rabbit, as she shut the oven door. 'Whatever has happened?' She looked anxiously at Tim who lay panting on the floor.

'Something came after me,' cried Tim, breathlessly.

'Something came after you?' echoed Mrs Rabbit. 'What was it like, my son?'

'It was very big and noisy,' replied Tim, with a shiver.

'It ran all round me, and tried to pull the coat off my back, and it snatched at my trousers.' He gave a sob, and his mother stroked his head.

'What did it say?' she asked. 'Did it speak or growl?'

'It called, "Whoo-oo-oo. Whoo-oo-oo. Whoo-oo-oo,"' whimpered the little rabbit.

'That was only the wind, my son,' said Mrs Rabbit, with a laugh. 'Never fear the wind, for he is a friend.' She gave the little rabbit a crust of new bread, and he was comforted.

The next day, when Tim Rabbit was nibbling a morsel of sweet grass under the hedge, the sky darkened, and a hail-storm swept across the sky, with stinging hail-stones. They bounced on the small rabbit and frightened him out of his wits. Off he ran, helter-skelter, with his white tail bobbing, and his eyes wide with fear. He lost his pocket handkerchief, and left his scarf in a thicket, but he hadn't time to pick them up, he was in such a hurry.

He raced and he tore towards the snug little house on the common, where his mother was tossing pancakes and catching them in her tiny stone frying-pan.

At last he reached the door, and in he raced without stopping to smooth his rough untidy hair.

'What's the matter, Tim?' asked Mrs Rabbit, as she put down her frying-pan. 'Whatever is the matter?'

'Something came after me,' exclaimed Tim, hiding behind her skirts.

'Something came after you?' cried Mrs Rabbit. 'What was it like?'

'It was big and dark,' said Tim. 'It threw hard stones at me, and hit my nose and back and ears. It must have a hundred paws, to throw so many stones, and every time it hit me and hurt me.'

'What did it say?' asked Mrs Rabbit, lifting her son from the floor, and straightening his ruffled hair.

'It shouted, "Whissh-ssh-ssh! Whissh-ssh-ssh!"' sobbed the little rabbit.

'That was only a hail-storm, Tim,' explained Mrs Rabbit. 'Never heed a hail-storm, for it clears the air, and makes all fresh for us rabbits.' She gave the little rabbit a curly yellow pancake with some sugar on the top, and he forgot his troubles.

The next day, when Tim was tasting an early primrose, the first he had seen in his short life, he had another fright. A thunder-storm broke out of the sky, with lightning which flashed around him, and peals of roaring thunder which echoed from the hills.

Tim scampered home as fast as his legs could carry him, to the warm little house on the common, where his mother was toasting currant teacakes in front of the wood fire.

At last he came to the door, and the smell of the teacakes made his whiskers twitch. He rushed inside, without stopping to shake the wet from his coat.

'What's the matter, Tim?' cried Mrs Rabbit, as he stumbled into a chair. She dropped her toasting-fork and leaned over him. 'What's the matter, my son?'

'Something came after me,' whispered Tim, shuddering.

'Something came after you?' echoed his mother. 'What was it like?'

'It was very big and high,' cried Tim. 'It stuck bright swords at me, and flashed lights in my eyes.'

'What did it say?' asked Mrs Rabbit softly.

'It roared "Roo-oo-oo-oo-oo-oo-oo!"' wept the little rabbit.

'That was only a thunder-storm, my son,' replied Mrs Rabbit, soothingly. 'Never mind the thunder and lightning. They never harmed a rabbit yet.' She gave him a large teacake, and he sat by the fire munching it, with his troubles forgotten.

But there came a day when Tim Rabbit sat dozing in a clump of ferns, half asleep, and comfortable. A gust of wind brought a queer scent to his nostrils and he awoke suddenly. He stared round and saw a strange animal bounding towards him with joyous leaps. It wasn't a lamb, nor a foal, nor a calf, nor even a pigling. It looked so playful and danced along so merrily on its four hairy legs that Tim wanted to play Catch, and Hide-and-seek.

What a jolly creature it was! How curly was its hair and its long waving tail! It hadn't seen Tim, for the ferns covered him, but he was prepared to run out and meet it. He would have invited it home with him, if a storm hadn't suddenly swept down from a dark cloud which hung in the sky.

'Beware! Beware!' howled the wind fiercely, and it blew Tim's fur the wrong way, so that he was uncomfortable and cold.

'Shoo! Shoo!' sighed the trees, waving their branches and crackling their twigs at him, like tiny wooden fingers.

'Run! Run!' cried the bushes, snapping and rustling their spiky boughs, with the prickly thorns.

'Be off! Be off!' roared the thunder, banging its drum inside the black cloud.

The lightning flashed and showed him the sharp teeth

of the merry dancing animal. The hailstones rattled down and hit foolish Tim's nose, so that he turned and ran, leaving the creature to play by itself in the wet field.

He scuttled towards the safe little house on the common, where his mother was making crab-apple tart. He ran in at the door, and flopped down on the oak bench.

'What's the matter, Tim?' asked his mother, dropping her rolling-pin and scattering the bowl of crab-apples. 'Whatever is the matter, my son?'

'Mother, I saw an animal. It was not a lamb, nor a foal, nor a calf, nor a pigling, but a lovely jumping animal. I was going to play with it, but the wind blew me, and the hailstones hit me, and the thunder scolded me, and they all drove me home.'

'What was it like, my son?' asked Mrs Rabbit, as she wiped the floor, and picked up her crab-apples.

'It was white, with kind eyes, and long ears and shining teeth, Mother, and its paws danced and pattered.'

'What did it say, Tim?' cried Mrs Rabbit, faintly.

'It said, "Bow-wow! Bow-wow!"'

'That was a dog, Tim,' whispered Mrs Rabbit, in a frightened tone. 'Beware of a dog! He would have killed you with his sharp teeth and pattering paws.'

So the little rabbit sat on his stool in the chimney corner, warming his toes by the fire, whilst he learned his first lesson:

'Crouch among the heather,
Never mind the weather,
Forget it altogether.
Run from a dog, a man, and a gun,
Or your happy young life will soon be undone.'

The Grandfather-clock and the Cuckoo-clock

ONE day the Grandfather rubbed his eyes, yawned, and climbed out of the grandfather-clock in the hall, where he had lived for two hundred years. The clock stopped ticking, the weights ran down, and there was silence.

He tripped lightly across the hall, drawing his old cloak around his shoulders, and pressing his tall hat on his head. He tapped at the tiny door in the carved wooden cuckoo-clock, hanging on the wall. The painted Cuckoo looked out, and then fluttered down to join him.

They slipped through the open window, and walked across the garden where the mignonette and poppies were blooming. Old Grandfather picked a sprig of lad's-love, which he stuck in his hat, and the Cuckoo flew up to his shoulder.

What a picture they made as they stood under the apple trees, sniffing at the sweet scents, listening to the birds, drinking the fragrant air! But no one saw them there.

'Let's go down the lane,' said the Grandfather, 'and see how the haymakers are getting on. I can smell the hay, and it's a hundred years since I was out.'

So down the lane they went, light as thistle-down, making no sound except their thin laughter.

In the meadows were babies tumbling over in the hay, and the haymakers tossed and raked the grass. A hay-cart, drawn by a great mare, came lumbering through the gate, laden with a heavy load.

Grandfather climbed up on the gate, and sat there swinging his legs, watching the men at work. But the little Cuckoo flew to a tree, and cuckooed twelve times.

'Oh ho!' cried Grandfather. 'Is it as late as that?' and he struck twelve with his deep ringing voice.

The haymakers put down their forks and rakes, and walked off to the hedge where their dinners lay in brown baskets under the dock leaves. The mare was set free from her load, and she whinnied her thanks to the strange pair.

Down jumped Grandfather and the Cuckoo, and they walked across the fields to the village school. They peeped through the open windows at the hot little children, sucking their pencils, frowning, wriggling, shuffling, as they struggled with their lessons.

'They ought to be out in the hay-field,' whispered the Grandfather to the Cuckoo.

So the Cuckoo called twelve times, and the Grandfather struck. All the children shut their books, and prepared to go home.

'My clock must be very slow!' murmured the teacher to herself. 'I had no idea it was so late.'

The scampering crowd ran past the old Grandfather with never a glance. They were looking for the Cuckoo, but he was so small, they never noticed his little coloured wings beating on a larkspur by the window.

Grandfather patted a fair little boy on the head, but he only shook his hair as if a wind had ruffled it, and ran after the others.

After them ran the Grandfather and the Cuckoo, but soon they left the children behind, hunting in the hedges, paddling in the streams, and away they went, through the village.

Leaning against a wall stood the policeman, and Grandfather stared at his fine helmet and bright buttons. But before he could speak the Cuckoo struck twelve again. Of course the Grandfather had to strike too, and his chimes rang through the village.

'Twelve o'clock!' exclaimed the policeman. 'I must get along to my dinner. Suet dumplings today,' and he hurried off home.

'I'm thirsty with all this striking,' cried the Cuckoo. 'Shall we go down to the river to bathe?'

'Yes,' replied the Grandfather. 'I want to see the old river again. I used to lie by its side when I was a boy, and dream, and dream.'

They walked through the uncut meadow grass, thick with dog-daisies and blue crane's-bill, to the great river. Grandfather's tight trousers were yellow with pollen, and the Cuckoo's wings were dipped in gold dust where he had fluttered among the flowers.

Then Grandfather sat down by the water's edge and

cooled his toes, and the Cuckoo flew over the surface, pretending to catch flies like the swallows.

The water-rats came swimming up to talk to them, and a family of white ducks paddled down a side stream from the farm to ask the news. Brown rabbits ran from their burrows and hopped on Grandfather's knee, and little water wagtails flirted their tails as they walked sedately up to pass the time of day.

A pair of dippers left their young ones to look at the odd couple on the bank, and a gay kingfisher darted across the river to Grandfather's feet.

'How is Time on the river, nowadays?' asked the Grandfather.

'It's much faster than when you lived here,' said the water-rat. 'We have to move so quickly, and work so hard, it is night soon after it is morning.'

'But it's more exciting,' said the ducks. 'You should see us cross the road and hold up the traffic!'

'Tell us of long ago time,' said the rabbits, and they crowded round him, as he sat among the purple loosestrife and creamy meadow-sweet by the river brink.

So he talked and talked, and the day slipped by. Presently a cool wind blew, and the sun dipped down towards the horizon. The ducks' feathers were ruffled and the water-rat turned up his collar.

'It's getting late,' said the Cuckoo, and he struck twelve. Grandfather chimed with his deep rich voice twelve times, too.

'Twelve o'clock?' cried the ducks. 'We shall be locked out all night, and the fox will catch us,' and they hurried off to the farm.

'Twelve o'clock?' cried the rabbits. 'What a joke!

But the weasels will get us if we don't go home,' and they scurried off to their burrows.

The dippers flew off to their lonely, wailing babies, and the kingfisher and wagtails hastened to their nests. Only the water-rats remained.

'The sun hasn't gone yet, I can see it winking at us. Your time must be wrong, Grandfather,' they said.

'Yes, we've been wrong all day,' answered the old Grandfather, as he reluctantly drew his toes out of the water.

'But it's been a holiday,' said the little Cuckoo. 'We left Time behind.'

Grandfather stooped to the meadow grass and picked a great dandelion clock, round and pearl-coloured. He blew and blew, and the water-rats and the Cuckoo watched him.

'Eight o'clock,' said he. 'It's time the children were in bed.'

So he said good-bye to the river, and waved to the water-rats, who sat on the bank watching him. With the Cuckoo on his shoulder, he ran through the bending grass, along the lanes, by the village, to the house which anxiously waited their return.

They climbed into their empty cases, and closed the doors. As soon as they were safely inside they both struck.

'One, Two, Three, Four, Five, Six, Seven, Eight.'

'Hello! The clocks are going again. They've stopped all day, and I couldn't make them go,' cried a voice.

'Time for bed, children.'

And, as the children went upstairs, the clocks sighed, and settled down to their quiet life again.

The Cornfield

It was a warm sweet-scented summer evening, and the moon and a few stars shone down on the fields, which lay like sheets of pale silver on the hillside. A hedgehog jogged along the country lane between the hedges, singing to himself his own little song of happiness.

> *'My lantern's the moon,*
> *My candle's a star,*
> *I travel by night,*
> *I wander afar.'*

He stamped his small feet in the dust in time to his thin high voice, and he felt the cool air in his prickles. A nightingale sang in the wood, but the hedgehog took no notice of its passionate music. He went on with his own song, singing so softly nobody but himself could hear it.

'My carpet's the moss,
My firelight the sun,
My house-roof the hedge,
When work is all done.'

It was a good song, he told himself, a traveller's song, and he was a hedgehog who couldn't abide staying at home. All day he had slept in his little bed of leaves, under the hedge, warmed by the hot sun, sheltered by tall ferns and velvety moss. Now night had come, and, in common with many small animals, he was wide awake, and off for a moonlight adventure.

He padded along the grassy verge of the lane, humming to himself, well content with life. Not far away stretched the broad smooth highway, the great road to London. Motor-cars and lorries whirled along with bright lights illuminating the hedges, spinning like gigantic golden-eyed animals, devouring all before them, and the hedgehog kept away from their roaring speed. They wouldn't follow him down the narrow rough lanes and the tiny green highways, under the arching meadow-sweet with its white, sweet flowers dipping to touch his back, and the forests of soft willow-herb. They couldn't hear the rustles among the leaves, or smell the flowers which attracted the white night-moths. He plodded cheerfully on, aware of every movement and smell around him.

He came at last to a gate, and against its bottom bar leaned an old Jack Hare.

'Hello, Jack,' said Hedgehog in his friendly way. 'How's the world treating you?'

'Pretty middling,' replied the hare, taking a straw from his mouth and turning round to the hedgehog.

'How's yourself?'

'Oh, pretty fairish,' said Hedgehog. 'It's a grand night.'

''Tis indeed! Where might you be going, Hedgehog?'

'Just over the fields to look at the corn a-growing. I allus likes to watch it grow. On a moonlight night it comes on a bit, and there's nothing like a cornfield to my thinking.'

'I'll come along with you,' said Jack Hare. 'I don't mind a bit of adventure. I've seen nobody all day but a couple of magpies, and a few rabbits, and a lost hen. I should like to see the corn a-growing.'

'There's a bright lantern hung in the sky tonight,' said Hedgehog as they ambled along together, the hare suiting his long steps to the short legs of the hedgehog. 'It gives a kind yellow light, that lantern aloft, not trying to the eyes like those twinkly lamps the farm men carry, or those terrible dazzlers on the motors.'

'I can't understand why they bother with those flashing lights when they've got a good lamp in the sky, that costs nothing and is held up for all the world to see,' said the hare. 'The ways of man are beyond me.'

'And me.' Hedgehog shook his little head and rattled his prickles in disdain, and very softly under his breath he sang his song.

'My lantern's the moon,
My candle's a star,
I travel by night
I wander afar.'

The two crossed a stream, the hare leaping it, the hedgehog paddling in the shallow water, and scrambling on the stones and twigs. By the water's edge, dipping his toes in the dark stream, sat a water-rat.

'How d'ye do?' said Hedgehog. 'How's life treating you?'

'Not so bad,' replied the water-rat. 'Where are you off to? Won't you stay here a while and cool yourselves in my brook? Come and look at the ripples I can make, and the waves all running away from my toes, one chasing another, like swallows in the air.'

'We're going over the fields to see the corn a-growing,' said Hedgehog, and the hare nodded and echoed: 'The green corn a-growing.'

'That's a pretty sight, and worth a journey,' agreed the water-rat. 'It does my heart good to see the corn a-sprouting and a-springing out of the ground, and waving its head. I'll come too if you don't mind. I've seen nothing all day but a couple of dilly-ducks, and a young frog. I'd like to see something sensible.'

They went along together, the hedgehog with his pointed snout and little bright eyes, humming his song, the hare with his great brown eyes glancing to left and right and behind him, and the water-rat with his sleek soft skin and little blunt nose. All the time the moon shone down with a bright silvery light, so that three little dusky shadows ran alongside the three animals.

They made a tiny track in the dewy grass, and they sipped the drops of pearly moisture from the leaves to quench their thirst. They passed a company of cows, lying near the path, and they saw a couple of farm horses cropping close to one another for company. Sweet scents of honeysuckle and briar came to them, and Hedgehog sang his little song once more.

A young hare was racing up and down in the moonlight, and Hedgehog called to him.

'Hello! young Hare,' said he. 'Why are you in such a hurry?'

The hare sat up, with his long ears twitching as he listened to the little sounds of night.

'I'm a bit mad,' said he. 'It's the moon. It makes me want to leap when I see that bright light. Can't stop, sorry!' and away he went, galloping over the pasture till he was out of sight.

'Poor fellow! I was just like that once,' said Jack Hare, 'but I've got a bone in my leg now.'

They reached a little knoll, and there they stopped, for in front of them stretched a field of golden wheat. It swayed gently as if an invisible hand stroked it, and even in the silence of the night a murmuring musical sound came from those million million ears of rustling corn.

The moon seemed to stand still in the sky, and look down at the wide cornfield, and the Great Bear blinked his eye and stared.

'Can you hear it muttering?' whispered the hedgehog. 'Can you hear the corn talking?'

'Is it alive like us?' asked the little water-rat.

'I can see it breathing, all moving as it takes a big breath,' said the hare. 'It's a wunnerful sight, a field of corn.'

'It's like water,' said the water-rat. 'It ripples and sighs and murmurs like the water in my brook at home.'

The great field with the tall slender stems of wheat growing thick and close, covering fifty acres, seemed to whisper, and the wheat-ears rubbed together as they swayed in the night air, and the sound was that of the sea, a low soft talk of myriad voices.

'This is my adventure,' said Hedgehog. 'I come here nearly every night, just to see the corn a-growing and a-blowing, and to listen to what it says.'

'It's a comforting homely talk,' said the hare, 'but I can't understand the language. I was never very good at languages. What does it say, Hedgehog?'

'Nay, I c-can't tell you exactly,' replied Hedgehog, hesitating, with his head aside, as he listened. 'I don't know the words, but they seem to me to be like a song. Listen. Now it's plainer.'

He held up his tiny fingered hand, and a myriad rustling voices sang:

> '*We are growing, growing, growing,*
> *The corn for the children's bread.*
> *The sap is flowing, flowing, flowing,*
> *From the roots unto the head.*
> *We are the corn,*
> *New-born,*
> *We make the bread.*'

The three animals sat breathless, listening to the little sounds and murmurs of the corn's voice. From the wood-side came the song of the nightingale, and overhead the moon and stars looked down.

'Aye, that's it!' said Hedgehog. 'That's what it tells you. It's growing, ripening, preparing for harvest. It's living, like us.'

They turned round and started off home again.

'Good night! Good night!' they said as they parted company. 'It was a grand sight. Something to remember.

We'll go again, all three of us, when the Harvest moon comes along. Good night.'

Hedgehog trundled home to his house-roof under the hedge, and Hare went back to the gate, but the little water-rat sat for a long time on the bank of his stream listening to the murmur of the water, and dreaming of the rustle of the corn.

The Merry-go-Round

HIGH up in the Chilterns there is a little village called Penn. The beech woods on the neighbouring hills surround it as a green and gold frame surrounds a picture. The old houses stand in a circle about the village green, eighteenth-century houses with brass knockers, and seventeenth-century houses with no knockers at all. People use their knuckles when they visit these small dwellings.

On the green there is a duck pond, where tiddlers live and water weeds grow. In the winter the children run from their homes and slide on the ice. They haven't any skates, and such things are not necessary, for they cost money. The children of Penn slide in their little strong boots, or they ride on the pond sitting in wooden boxes from the small grocer's shop which is also the post office. Some even sit on tea-trays from their mothers' kitchens. They are wrapped in gay scarves and they shout till their voices ring like the church bells in the cold air.

In spring they catch each other as they race over the green and run round the trees. In summer they fish for minnows, with bent pins and pieces of string. In autumn they watch the golden leaves fly down from the trees, and they stretch out their hands to grab them. Every autumn leaf caught before it touches the earth brings good luck, as all country folk know.

Every year in September there is a Fair on the green. That is something to look forward to. The caravans and lorries laden with strange and exciting things come puffing up the long hill from the small town in the valley. Women wearing gold ear-rings sit at the doors of the yellow caravans, and look out at the beech woods through which they ride, keeping an eye for a rabbit or maybe a fat pheasant on the way. Men lead the piebald horses, and lurchers run behind or dart into the hedges. Motor-vans bring the heaviest gear, hidden away and locked up, but round the sides of the vans there are painted notices to say the horses and roundabouts are within.

Everybody is on the look-out for the Fair people, who come past the old grey church on the hill-top, and sweep round the great elm tree which is a landmark, and down the road by the little stream to the village green and its houses.

At the Red House facing the green, the twins, John and Michael, are the most excited of all, for they know that the Fair will be just outside their windows. They can watch it as they eat their porridge in the morning, and at night they go to sleep with the rapturous noise of the merry-go-round ringing in their ears. They hear the talk of the shows, and when a woman wearing a gold chain comes to the back door for a jug of hot water, they rush to get it for her.

The shooting ranges and the side-shows are soon set up, and the women in the caravans make fires on the green and do a little washing. They carry buckets of water from the village pond, and boil it, and wash their clothes in the open air. Then they put clothes-lines between the caravans and hang their garments up to dry. It is a busy time, and the women like to get the chance of plenty of water and no crowds.

The platform of the merry-go-round is set up, with the silvery trumpets and glass reflectors in the centre. The men lift the horses from the great van, and carry them to the gilded poles. They slip them in the sockets, and go back for more. It takes a long time to put the lovely horses in their places, and the children all stand near to watch.

One Fair day a strange thing happened, and John and Michael still wonder if it were real or a dream. But two boys cannot have the same dream at the same time, and besides, there is the little whistle to be accounted for.

The Fair had come as usual that September day, and the boys had been out to watch the caravans arrive and to give a hand to the man at the coconut-shy, setting up the white wooden bottles – for, of course, as it was during the war, there were no coconuts. They knew most people in the Fair, and they went to visit the old woman who was the grandmother of some of the showmen, and the great-grandmother of others. She sat at the door of her red and gold caravan, a woman incredibly old, her face dark brown, wrinkled like a wizenedy apple, her black eyes sparkling with hidden fires, her hands like claws.

'How are you, Mrs Lee?' asked John.

'Are you quite well, Mrs Lee?' asked Michael.

She turned her sharp gaze upon the two boys, recognizing them at once.

'Not so good, my dears. Only middling,' said she.

'We've brought something for you, Mrs Lee,' said John.

'My mother sent it,' added Michael, and he put a little basket of cakes and honey and an egg in the old woman's hand.

'And this,' said John, dropping a rose on the top.

'Thank you, my dears. God bless you and your mother, and Good Luck be with you,' said Mrs Lee, spreading out the contents of the basket on her white apron. Then she hobbled into the caravan to put them away, and returned with something in her tight fist.

She called to them. 'Hi! My dears! Come here! I've got summat for you too. You'll always remember old Hepzibah Lee. She's got summat for you.'

Mrs Lee held out a small shining object, and John took it.

'It's a whistle,' said he. 'Oh, just what I wanted.'

'Nay, don't 'ee blow it now,' cried Mrs Lee, as he put it to his lips. 'It's summat special. It's made of bronze. I fun' it once-on-a-time, when I was burying summat in a wood. I cleaned it up. It's very old, older nor me. It's Roman they say.'

Michael and John stared at the tiny bronze whistle, which was in the shape of a dolphin, with the lips for the mouth of the whistle, and the tail at the end.

'Thank you. Thank you very much, Mrs Lee,' said Michael, and he ran off with John at his side to take the basket back to the Red House, and to show the wee whistle to his mother.

They blew the little whistle, and a strange sweet note came from it, very small, very shrill and clear as a bell. Down by the pond the horses from the Fair were being watered.

They lifted their heads and neighed in reply. The boys blew the whistle again, and there was a faint shrill whinny from somewhere else. It may have been a horse in the field behind the cottages, or a wooden horse on the merry-go-round, or even a silver horse flying in the air, invisibly galloping out of the clouds – who knows when magic is about?

The engine puffed and the travelling-band began to move, the merry-go-round went slowly round. The people came down the road, and the Fair was open. It was dull and quiet till night, when the crowds from all the villages for miles came, but the afternoon was given up to children.

John and Michael took their pennies, and chose their favourite horses. They stood watching the merry-go-round, and two horses seemed more beautiful than the others. Their names, printed in curly letters on their necks, were Hot Fun and Spit Fire. They had scarlet saddles, and their backs were painted in green and blue and cherry-red, with diamonds of scarlet and scrolls of gold. Their mouths were open, showing white teeth and red tongues that lolled out. Their gold eyes flashed, their heads were thrown back in the speed of their running. They looked very magnificent.

The boys rode on these two all afternoon, until their money was spent. It was grand to career on these galloping horses, with their red nostrils and their carved golden manes. John stooped over his steed and patted its neck at the end of each ride, and Michael stroked the hard flank of his hobby-horse. Did they both feel a tremor in the wood, as their hands lingered there? They secretly thought so, but perhaps it was the vibration of the engine, or even the noise of the music blaring 'Daisy, Daisy, Give me your answer do', from the bright silvery trumpets under the reflecting mirrors in the centre.

At last all the money had gone, and the two boys reluctantly went home to tea.

'I could ride for ever like that,' sighed John. 'I hope when I'm grown up I shall go on liking it.'

'Of course you will,' said his mother. 'Tonight there will be many grown-up people enjoying the horses, just like you.'

'Not quite as much,' said Michael. 'They don't really believe when they're grown up.'

They went out again in the evening to the Mystery Cave, and the Haunted House, and they spent a few more pennies there, but so many lads were coming from the farms there was no chance to get another ride on the two famous horses, Hot Fun and Spit Fire. Other people, who knew nothing of the feelings of those horses, rode on their backs when the stars came in the sky and the moon looked down.

'Good night, Hot Fun. Good night, Spit Fire,' said the boys, and away they went back home to supper and to bed.

It was splendid to lie there and to listen to the music of the merry-go-round, and the Fun Fair, to hear the shouts and the laughter. They lay in their little room, listening, and talking, and then they slept.

The sounds grew quieter, the last bus went away, the last people called 'Good night', and the showmen shut their booths and extinguished their flares.

It must have been two o'clock in the morning when Michael awoke and looked out of the window. He could see the wooden horses like ghosts, very still and pale under the moon. Here and there a glimmer of light shone from a hanging lantern. A dog barked, a horse grunted at its picket, and a splash came from the pond as something touched the water. A white owl flew over, and strange and delicious smells of foreign people, of gipsies, and horses and fair grounds came in at the window, mingled with the late honeysuckle on the front of the house.

Michael could see the old gipsy woman's caravan, and a glow in the window.

'Old Mother Lee is awake too,' he thought and then he remembered the whistle. He fetched it from his trouser pocket and leaning from the window he blew a little blast on it.

Up leapt John, pattering to his side.

'Whatever are you doing, Michael? Can you see something?' he asked.

'Look! Look!' cried Michael excitedly. 'Look at the horses, John.' He blew again on the bronze whistle.

Under the moon they saw that those galloping horses, fixed in their places, were moving. They were going round the circle, swinging up and down, and spinning slowly around the mirrors and silver trumpets. The engine was still, they went by themselves. There was faint music too, so soft that they could hardly hear it, but of course it might have been the wind blowing through the trees. It wasn't playing 'Daisy, Daisy, Give me your answer do', but something else, wild, sweet and strange.

'Come along out. Put your coat on over your pyjamas. Let's slip out and have a ride for nothing,' whispered John.

They put on their dressing-gowns and bedroom slippers, and crept downstairs to the hall. In a moment they unbolted the door and stood in the porch. Another step, and they were out on the village green.

They ran across the damp trampled grass to the merry-go-round. There was no doubt, it was moving more quickly now, swinging in its circle, with nobody riding. The horses looked like silver phantoms gliding softly through the air, up and down, as the platform revolved. The boys waited a moment, reading the names as the horses passed, and each horse moved its head and stared at them with eager eyes. Then came Spit Fire and Hot Fun. They climbed on the platform and sprang on the horses.

'They are real,' cried John, as he felt the warm flesh under his knees, and his hands touched the smooth skin of Spit Fire's neck. Spit Fire quivered and shook its mane. The gold hair was thick and harsh, blowing in the wind.

'They are alive,' whispered Michael, and his horse, Hot Fun, turned its head and gave a faint whinny of recognition.

The horses went very quickly, they whirled round, they danced on their outstretched hooves, they pawed the air, and neighed in high shrill tones. They swung and reared and bucked and the boys clung to the reins, not knowing whether to be rather frightened or to be filled with exhilaration and joy. After their first surprise they enjoyed it more than anything they had ever known.

Then Michael blew his whistle, just a little blow at it, in the excitement. The cool high note flew out under the moon, and the horses all tossed their heads and whinnied back. Down from the platform they leapt, down on to the village green, and the boys held tightly to their horses' necks, lest they should be thrown.

'Goodness, Spit Fire! Where are you going?' asked John.

'Hot Fun, what's the matter?' cried Michael.

The horses galloped across the grass, between the caravans and past the booths to the duck pond. They all dipped their heads and drank the water. Six-and-thirty little horses were there, encircling the pond. How deeply they drank! They were very thirsty, for they had not tasted water for a long time.

Then one horse swung round and galloped across the green, and another followed, till all of them were off. They went along the road, and their little hooves made such a clatter one would think everybody would have been wakened by them. Their stiff gold manes shone in the moonlight, their bright eyes glistened as the horses looked sideways and shied at the moon shadows.

Gallop! Gallop! Gallop! they went, and then they sobered down and began to trot.

Trot! Trot! Trot! they went all along the white road.

Michael and John were breathless with the excitement of that night ride. They held their reins tightly, and kicked with their heels and pressed the horses' sides with their knees. Their old dressing-gowns floated behind them like wings, their hair was on end, but, although they might have been cold, they felt the warmth of their steeds under them, and the beating of hearts.

Gallop! Gallop! went the horses again, and they careered past the old grey church, with its lych-gate on the top of the hill. The ancient tombstones were criss-crossed with moonlight, and the yew trees were dead black. Past the school they went, round by the Crown Inn, with its roses and ivy on its mullions, and down to the valley and the woods.

There, under the beech trees, they stopped, and the boys got off. The horses pushed their way into a field and began to eat the sweet grass.

'It's Farmer Pennington's field,' said Michael.

'There's his mare, watching us,' said John.

The white mare was staring at this company of six-and-thirty little horses. She shook her head and whinnied loudly, and they all replied in their own language. She came slowly across, and nuzzled them with her nose. The boys sat on a gate and watched her. She had a word with every one of those little horses, but what she said I cannot tell. It was a secret among them all.

Then Michael blew his little whistle, and what a commotion there was! The little horses came cantering three abreast, and the two boys only just managed to catch the reins and leap up on the backs of Spit Fire and Hot Fun before they went out to the road.

Away they went, back to the Fair. The moon had gone, the fields and the churchyard were misty in the milk-white air of dawn. The corncrake was calling in the barley field, and the yaffle flew over. The little horses scampered down the road to the green. They leapt up to the empty platform, and climbed to their places.

John and Michael clambered down, and patted their horses' necks. The horses were breathing quickly, and steam rose from them.

'I hope they won't get cold,' said John. 'We ought to rub them down, really.'

They stood for a few minutes, and even as they waited the horses were turned back to wood, their wild life was calmed, and they stayed stiffly in their places, with no breath or motion.

'Good night, Spit Fire. Good night, Hot Fun,' called the boys. Then they tucked up their dressing-gowns and ran back to the house. The door was ajar as they had left it. They went upstairs to bed, tossing their soaking slippers on the carpet, throwing their damp dressing-gowns on the floor.

'Give one more blow at the whistle,' said John, as they looked through the window at the Fair.

Michael put his hand in the dressing-gown pocket. The whistle had gone!

'It must have fallen out when we sat on the gate,' said he, sadly.

'No, you had it after that,' said John. 'You must have lost it when we got off the horses, at the end. We will look for it tomorrow.'

The merry-go-round stood still, the silver horses were dusky in the mist. A light was shining in Mrs Lee's caravan.

'She's been waiting for the horses to come back,' said John.

'I expect she knew all about it,' agreed Michael.

They were very sleepy the next day, and their mother was puzzled over their damp slippers and some rents in their dressing-gowns. Briars and burrs were stuck to the wool, and silver horsehairs were on their pyjamas.

'Oh, we had a great adventure!' they cried. 'We went riding in the middle of the night.'

'Riding?' echoed their mother. 'In the night?'

'Riding on the roundabout horses, Mother. We went off to Farmer Pennington's field and the horses drank from the pond, and ate the grass.'

'Which horses? You've been dreaming, my dears.'

'The little hobby-horses, of course. When we blew the whistle, Mother. But we lost it.'

'Then go and look for it, John and Michael,' said their mother. 'It was a beautiful whistle.'

They hunted high and low, but they couldn't find it. All day the merry-go-round whirled, and the horses cantered in their circle, but there was no little whistle to set them free. The boys rode on Spit Fire and Hot Fun, but there was no beating heart, or answering whinny.

Early the next day the Fair went away. The vans were loaded, the merry-go-round was packed, and the great engines puffed and snorted and dragged them along the road, across the green, past the pond, and far away.

Then Michael saw something shining in the grass. He stooped and picked up the little bronze whistle.

Quickly he blew it. From far up the road came an answering call. All the little horses, packed in the van, whinnied back in shrill tiny cries of recognition, and the piebald ponies and horses of flesh and blood drawing the caravans also whinnied.

Old Mrs Lee was sitting at the door of her red and gold caravan at the end of the procession looking over the bottom door. She waved her brown hand to the little boys.

'I see you've been a-blowing yon whistle,' she called.

'Thank you! Yes, Mrs Lee!' they replied.

'Good Luck, and God bless you,' she cried, as the caravan lurched away.

'God bless you, too,' called the boys, and that was the last they saw of her.

The Fair comes every year, and they blow the whistle, but Mrs Lee is no longer in her caravan, and the little wooden horses never leave their places in the ring. However, someday, someday, who knows what may happen?

The Red Hen

In the cottage down our lane lived an old woman who was quite alone in the world. She had neither kith nor kin, for she had outlived them all. She worked from morning till night, keeping her cottage clean, digging in her small garden, and making little mats which she sold. Her tin mugs gleamed like silver, and her brass candlestick shone like gold, but that was all the gold and silver she possessed unless you count the goldy-locks which bloomed in her garden and the silver pence of the bright honesty which grew close to the cottage wall.

In summer days she put a chair in the doorway and sat there sewing and pegging the coloured rags into the little round mats, and then she could talk to the passers-by; but when winter came she took her work indoors and sewed by the wood fire. Then it was she wished for company.

'If only I had a somebody to talk to,' said she to herself. 'If only I had a body to share my cup of milk and bite of bread, to crack a joke with me, and tell a tale, then I should be set up!'

She sighed and held her needle close to the candle and threaded it with the coarse linen thread. Then she put on her stout old thimble and went on with her work.

'Yes, it would be grand, but I couldn't keep a body. I've only just enough to manage. It's hard work digging my garden, and tending my 'tater patch, and picking up sticks in yonder wood.'

She was a brave old woman, and she kept her home together, struggling against ill health and poverty. She always had a smile for the passer-by and a flower or cutting from her garden.

One night, when she had uttered her wish for company, she heard a faint tap, tap on the door. It was such a soft little fluttering sound she thought it was only the leaves blown from the path, or a loose branch of her rose-bush, but when the tapping went on, she got up and opened the door a crack.

At first she could see nobody, for it was a dark night, and her candle blew out as she stood in the doorway. Then she heard a cluck close to the ground, and she spied a little hen, crouched in a bunch on the step.

'Come in out of the cold, little hen,' she cried, stooping to lift it, for she feared it was hurt or lost. The little hen leapt over her hands and walked sedately into the house right up to the fire, where it perched itself on the creepie stool.

'La!' cried the old woman. 'Here's a visitor indeed, sitting down on my stool as free and easy as a trooper!'

'Cluck! Cluck!' replied the little hen, and it puffed out its wet red feathers and preened itself in the fire's glow.

The old woman bustled about preparing supper. She crumbled some bread in a saucer and poured hot water and a drop of milk over it to soak it. The little hen watched every movement and it ate its supper hungrily.

'Poor little thing! You were well-nigh famished,' said the old woman. She stroked the hen, and it was as thin as a rake. 'Deary me! You look as if you had had no food for days.'

She filled up the hen's saucer from her own supper-mug, and the bird clucked softly, as if to thank her. It jumped down to the floor and nestled in the corner by her chair. When the old woman began to make her rugs the little hen watched, and in a minute it tried to help. It saw her take a little strip of coloured rag from a basket on the hearth, and peg it into a cloth. So the little hen picked out the strips and held them up to her. It was a most obliging little hen!

The clock struck nine, and it was time for bed. The old woman lined a box with a piece of her red flannel petticoat and put it on the hearthstone, in the corner away from the heat of the fire.

'There, little red hen! You can go to sleep when you've a mind,' said she, lifting the thin little bird into the cosy nest.

And there it lay, with its golden eye watching her, and its red feathers gently moving in the comfort of its new home. The old woman was herself preparing for bed when there was a loud rap! rap! at the door.

'Dear me! More visitors?' she cried, and she slipped on her skirt and unbolted the door.

On the doorstep stood a dark rough man with a knife in his hand.

'Have you seen a little red hen?' he asked.

'What if I have?' said the old woman defiantly.

'It's mine!' said the man gruffly, and he stepped indoors without waiting to be invited and looked about him.

'There it is, on your hearthstone! Yes, that's my hen right enough, strayed away and I've been looking for it. But it shan't go off again, for I'm going to kill it for dinner tomorrow.'

'Oh, please don't,' cried the old woman, quickly shielding the frightened little red hen. 'Please leave it. It's such a thin little hen.'

'That's true,' agreed the man with a laugh. 'It won't make much of a dinner.'

He looked cunningly at the old woman and asked, 'What will you give me for it? It would fatten up, but I've no time to bother over it, for it runs away and hides every night, and it's never yet laid an egg. What will you give me for it?'

Now the old woman had only a few pence and that wasn't enough to buy a hen. She looked round the room and hesitated, and the man stared at her bits of furniture, and the rag rugs on the stone floor. It was a bare little room, with nothing much left from the days of her old happiness.

'I'll take that brass candlestick,' said the man, pointing to the candlestick in the old woman's hand. 'My missis has always pestered me to buy one, although I tell her that brass has to be cleaned. That's a nice one, and I'll take that for the hen.'

The old woman's hand trembled as she held out the candlestick. It was her last treasure, the reminder of days gone past, and it had held her candle for fifty years, and borne the little conical extinguisher, like a nightcap, hooked in its side.

'Yes, I'll let you have my brass candlestick for the poor little hen's life,' said she slowly.

'Well, I shall be right glad to get rid of that roving fowl,' grinned the man, 'and this is a rare candlestick. I think I've got the best of the bargain. Good night, missis.'

He opened the door and stalked out into the darkness. The little old woman looked down at the red hen, snuggled in the warm box.

'Good night, little red hen,' said she softly, and she crept upstairs in the dark.

The next morning she found the kitchen swept, and a good fire burning. The table was set for breakfast and the kettle filled with fresh water from the spring in the yard. On the tablecloth lay a brown egg for the old woman's breakfast.

'Bless you, my dear!' she cried, holding up her hands in astonishment. 'Here's a red fairy I've got in the house!'

The little red hen clucked and ruffled its feathers. Then it flew to a chair and sat waiting for its portion of crumbs.

'Where did you learn to do all these things?' asked the old woman, but the little red hen answered never a word.

'You are such a clever little hen, I'm glad your master sold you to me. Eat you, indeed! You're a marvel, that you are!'

After breakfast the old woman washed the cup and teapot, and the little red hen busied itself about the house. It was most wonderful to see how well the little fowl worked. It was so quick and neat and so thoughtful, the old woman had her housework finished in no time at all. The little hen baked the bread, and polished the tin mugs and spoons, while the old woman sat in the rocking chair, warming her toes by the clean hearth.

'I've never seen a wee body as quick and clever as you, my dear little crittur,' said she.

In the afternoon they went for a walk in the woods. The old woman hobbled along in her grey shawl, and the little red hen ran by her side, peeping at this and that with its quick-searching eyes. Many a curious pebble and flower and stick it brought to her, and she laughed at the way it flew here and there, excited and gay. The birds looked down and sang to the little hen. The squirrels chattered to it, but it danced along its way in the old woman's company.

The old woman picked up sticks and gathered a bundle which she carried under her arm. Of course, the hen couldn't help in this heavy work, but it peered about and discovered the broken boughs and led her to them, saving her from wandering in search of the firewood. Then home they went to have tea, with the wood crackling in the hearth, and the new bread fresh from the oven.

The old woman fetched her work-basket and began to mend a tear in her skirt. The little hen picked up the needle and thread, and darned the work with the smallest stitches. Then the old woman made a little apron and tied it round the hen's waist to keep its feathers clean, and she stitched a grey cloak for it to wear in wintry weather. She found a tiny plate and dish, put away from her own childhood toys, and these she brought out for the little hen's pleasure.

But the little red hen was seldom idle, and when the old woman brought home some sewing to do for the lady at the big house, the hen seized the needle and did the work. It featherstitched in the most delicate way, and embroidered with tiny dots and dashes, and put on the buttons and sewed the button holes in a manner the old woman with her tired eyes never could have managed. After that there was a supply of sewing to be done, from baby clothes to shirts for the gentlemen, and everyone wondered at the delicate stitchery of the old dame who lived alone in the cottage with her red hen for company.

Money began to fill the old woman's purse, and she had many a little luxury of honeycomb and blanket and new white mutch for her hair. No longer had she to fear poverty, for the little red hen with her stitches brought comfort to the cottage, and by her cheerful presence kept the old woman happy.

'If only you could talk, my dear,' said she to the hen. And the little red hen clucked and shook its little head.

One day when they were out walking, the old woman in her new scarlet cloak and the little red hen with its feathers brushed and sparkling, they met the cruel man who had once owned the hen. When he saw it so plump and so happy, with feathers shining like gold and eyes bright as stars, he wanted that hen back again.

At night he went to the cottage and knocked at the door.

'Who's there?' called the old woman, and the little red hen flew down from the creepie stool and hid inside the flour sack.

'It's someone to bring you good fortune,' said the man at the door.

The old woman unlocked it and he came inside.

'I want to buy back my red hen,' said he.

'But I'm not willing to sell her,' said the old woman.

'Come! What will you take?' wheedled the man. 'I'll give you anything in reason, for I've set my heart on having that hen.'

The old woman shook her head.

'And I've set my heart on keeping her,' said she. 'It's idle to stay talking. Good night to you, sir.'

She held the door open, but the man frowned and blustered. Then he took a purse from his pocket and threw a piece of gold on the table.

'There!' said he. 'What do you say to that?'

'No. I won't part with her. Not for all the gold in your purse. She's my friend now.'

The man shook his fist angrily and looked round as if he would carry off the little hen in spite of the old woman, but the bird was nowhere to be seen.

'Where have ye hidden that hen?' shouted the man, and he shook the old woman's arm and turned over the work-basket and looked under the table. There was no little red hen to be seen and, grumbling at the magicky wickedness of the creature, he stamped out of the house.

Then the little red hen came hopping out of the flour sack shaking herself, and her feathers were so white it took half an hour for her to get rid of the flour. At the keyhole stooped the man, and he nodded and muttered as away home he went.

The next night he returned with his purse and his demands.

As soon as the old woman heard his step she beckoned to the little hen who leapt into the flour sack and hid.

'No. I won't sell my little red hen,' said the old woman, sternly.

'Where is my hen? Where have you hidden her?' asked the man, and he kept one eye on the flour sack in the corner.

'Find her if you can,' said the old woman.

'I've a fancy for your flour sack,' said he, and he seized the sack and carried it off in a twinkling before the little hen could squeak out.

Away he carried her, to his own house over the hill, and he dropped the sack in the kitchen.

'We've got that little red hen,' said he to his wife, 'and now we'll find out what is the magicky thing about her. Either she lays golden eggs, or she has rubies under the wings or something else unnatural.'

'I always knew there was some queer happenings because she was off hunting and peering and peeping when she lived here,' said his wife. 'And think of the royal egg-shell she came from!'

'She never laid an egg for us, but I stole two from the old woman's dresser, when she wasn't looking. If they are gold, we'll keep the hen. If they aren't, we'll eat her.'

So they took the little hen out of the flour sack, and looked under her feathers for rubies or pearls, but there was nothing. Then they broke the eggs the man had stolen, and they were only ordinary hen eggs, with yellow yolks and no gold at all.

'Did you ever find out what that little blue stone was that we found in the red hen's nest one day?' asked the husband.

'No value at all! Not worth a penny!' said the wife,

crossly. 'It's in that broken teapot, and the egg-shell is with it. We've had no luck with this hen ever since it came out of that shell with a crown on it. I thought it was something special when the gipsy sold me the egg, but out came a very small chicken, and it has become a little hen, no good at all. It has only brought us trouble, running away and hiding and all.'

'We will eat it tomorrow. It will make a good dinner, for the old woman has fed it up. I'll roast it, I will, and stuff it and serve it with bread sauce and gravy, I will.'

'Mind it doesn't get away tonight. Leave it in the house, and tie its legs together.'

The little red hen, lying on the floor with her legs tied, heard all they said. When the man and his wife were in bed the hen shuffled over the floor and managed to flutter up to the broken teapot on the dresser. Inside lay the silver-blue stone and the egg-shell. The stone was the size of a grain of wheat. The hen had looked for it high and low, for it was her voice, which she had lost. The egg-shell had a golden crown upon it.

She swallowed the little blue stone, and immediately her voice returned to her. The egg-shell she put under her wing.

Then, with her new voice, she called, and the sound of it went through the air and roused all the cocks and hens in the country for miles. The hens cackled on their perches, and nudged the cocks at their sides.

'The Queen's voice! The red hen is in danger,' they whispered.

Then off flew the cocks, over the hills and along the valleys, crowing as they went, waking other cocks at farms and cottages on the way. They all came to rescue the little red hen who was in distress. They pecked with their sharp beaks and tore with their spurs and they crowed like bedlam let loose.

One picked the lock and another broke the windows. One unfastened the string round the little red hen's feet and another led her to the door. Away flew the little red hen with the brass candlestick under her wing back to the old woman's house, but the cocks had not finished. They blew the soot from the chimney over the room, and fluttered against the pots and pans and sent them rolling. They beat their wings up and down to cause as much disorder as possible.

'Whatever is the matter?' cried the man, leaping from bed.

'Burglars about,' said his wife. 'Don't go downstairs.' But the man crept down and opened the door. At him flew the great cocks; they knocked the candle from his hand and pecked him and buffeted him till he ran upstairs again.

'They've got spears and daggers, and they beat me with heavy cudgels,' he cried, all trembling. 'Surely they are the powers of darkness let loose by that wicked little red hen!'

They both lay under the bedclothes listening to the shrill cockadoodles that rent the air.

When at last it was quiet, the two ventured downstairs.

What a scene of confusion there was! The kitchen was topsy-turvy, with dishes broken on the floor and soot and cinders everywhere.

'Just as I thought!' grunted the man. 'The little red hen has gone. She's the cause of all this!'

'And she has taken the candlestick and that little stone

and broken egg-shell,' said his wife. 'Never mind. The candlestick can go, for I was tired of cleaning it, and I expect the hen was tough. But the mess! I wish you had never brought her back here again, husband. She was always a trouble to us.'

'Never again,' said her husband. 'She can stay at the old woman's house till she's as old as Methuselah and I won't bother about her. If she had laid golden eggs, it would be different, but she isn't worth a penny piece.'

The little red hen stepped through the hole which the old woman had cut for her in the cottage door, and went to her bed by the fireside. When the old woman came down in the morning, there was great rejoicing.

'My dear little red hen!' cried the old woman. 'I heard such a cockadoodling in the night I was sure somebody was trying to rescue you. How did you get home again? But of course you can't tell me.'

'Oh, yes, I can,' said the little red hen in a husky, dusky voice. 'I found my voice. It was in the broken teapot, hidden away with the royal egg-shell of my birth. Now I can tell you everything.'

And the little red hen sat down with the old woman and they told one another tales. The old woman's tales were about the boys and girls she had known in her long life, and the Christmas parties and birthday treats and marriages and christenings she had attended. The little red hen's stories were about the fairy folk and witches and dwarfs and goblins she had met in her own time as the Queen of them all. Both the little red hen and the old woman enjoyed the tales so much they never stopped chattering to one another.

So the little red hen stayed with the old woman to be her comfort and her companion all the rest of her life, and when at last the old woman died at the age of a hundred and one, a little red hen was carved on her tombstone. But our little red hen flew off to try to get to Paradise too.

The Tom Tit and the Fir Tree

Little Tom Tit and tall Fir Tree
Sang a carol joyously.
Tom Tit whistled with elfin might,
The stars peeped down to see the sight.
Fir Tree waved his plumes serene,
Plucked his harp with fingers green,
Sang to the Holy Ones above,
A Christmas carol of Peace and Love.
Frost and glitter on meadow and lea,
Little Tom Tit and tall Fir Tree.

'THERE!' cried the Tom Tit, as he stopped to take breath. 'That's as grand a music as ever came out of this wood. The oaks and the great beeches couldn't do better. I should think the sound of it has gone twice round the world. What do you think, Fir Tree? Wasn't it a splendid music that we made?'

The tall Fir Tree nodded his shaggy head, and sighed in the wind, and the murmur of his sighing was like the roaring of the sea.

'The stars are out, Tom Tit,' he boomed in his deep voice. 'Orion the Hunter is climbing the sky with his belt all a-glitter. The Dog Stars are racing around, and there's the Hare crouching before them. The Great Bear is prowling in the fields of heaven, and Aldebaran is winking his red eye. It's dangerous for a little bird like you to be abroad. You'd best be off to bed, Tom Tit.'

The little blue tit swung lightly on the bough, and peeked up impudently at the Great Bear marching in the night sky. That furry golden Bear would never catch *him*, for it moved so slowly only the solemn old Fir Tree could see its motion, and of course the tree watched all through the winter, whereas the Tom Tit could fly away like blue lightning.

'Be off to bed, young Tom Tit. It is Christmas Eve, and mysteries are abroad,' bellowed the Fir Tree, as the wind caught it and tossed its boughs. 'Birds and beasts should be a-bed, and the trees will watch the sky alone tonight.'

Tom Tit crept into an ivy bush, and put his head under his wing in the warm shelter of the large thick leaves. Then he fell asleep, but every now and then he awoke, and opened one bright eye to peer about like a child who wants to catch Santa Claus, for the Tom Tit wished to get a glimpse of the happenings that the Fir Tree had told him about. It was the Holy Night, the Fir Tree said, and a star travelled across the sky bringing tidings of joy, and all the heavens sang, just as Fir Tree and Tom Tit had carolled together. So the Tom Tit put his head from under his wing and kept his beady eye on the dark-blue sky, watching.

The earth appeared to be sleeping, but in reality it was more watchful than in the daytime. Every blade of grass in the wide pastures, every leafless tree in the wood, moved softly, stretching upward and then bowing down.

The Fir Tree stood very straight and majestical, with its dark branches vibrant, as it looked at the wonders, and the little Tom Tit gazed entranced.

He saw the moon sail along the sky like a splendid ship and on deck there was a host of shining angels with trumpets and horns, singing and playing the heavenly music, cold and clear and far away. The ship moved through the blue air, journeying to some unknown port.

Meteorites shot down, leaving long trails of gold, until they disappeared among the darkly watching trees of the woods on the horizon. The Tom Tit saw the twinkling changing colours of the great stars, but the Fir Tree hailed them as his friends. They were the familiar winter stars, great Aldebaran, and blue Rigel, the Bull with his round eye, and the prancing Goat, Capella. The Fir Tree knew them all like his own sisters and brothers in the fir wood, for ever since he was a seedling tree he had whispered to them in the night, watching for them to appear above the sky-line.

Across the dome above him swept the broad band of the Milky Way, a white pathway of stars, and the Fir Tree could see the millions of worlds like silver sand which made it. Down that pale road came a company of angels, flying towards the earth, singing as they came, and the sound of their voices, thin and sweet, was mingled with the nearer music of the host on the slowly sailing ship of the moon.

The Fir Tree turned away from these and searched the skies for something else. He stared towards the east, longingly, and the little Tom Tit leaned from his ivy shelter to look too. Suddenly the Fir Tree saw what he had waited for ever since he and the little bird had sung their carol. Out of the blue depths came a star with five points, brilliant, moving rapidly. It was the Star of Bethlehem which appears each Christmas Eve in memory of the First Christmas.

It travelled across the jewelled sky and came to rest over the great square tower of the old church in the village. There it hung like a lantern to guide wanderers home, and every stone in the tower shone under its light. After it came the moonship with its angel passengers, and the moon dropped its anchor in the churchyard. Then all the little angels came fluttering out, and some of them perched on the tower, and stayed there, round-faced and rosy-winged cherubs. Others entered the church, for every window and door was wide open, and a radiance came from within.

Although the Fir Tree never moved, for his roots went deep among the rocks of the earth, yet he could see the scene inside the holy place as clearly as if he were there. But the little Tom Tit sprang from his shelter and flew like a blue arrow to the doorway, where he hid behind the carving and watched.

The cherubs rustled their rosy wings and floated up the aisle to the altar, and all the tall angels from the Milky Way followed after them, with never a sound, except the music of their voices. There lay a little Babe in a cradle of straw, and His wide-open eyes looked up at His visitors, who floated around like the snowflakes of a celestial snowstorm, pure and cold and beautiful.

Through the open door streamed more and more angels, as the Milky Way gave up its myriads of travellers. The music grew louder and the angels adored the little One lying there, while from the woods came a rustling and murmuring as the trees joined in the praise.

Then an astonishing thing happened. There was a flutter of earthly wings and a beating of the air, and through the church came a flock of birds. They perched on the altar, and filled the choir stalls, where on Sundays rosy-faced boys from the cottages sat demure with white surplices covering their best Sunday clothes. The birds looked like choirboys, with their round heads and bright eager eyes and chattering tongues. There were thrushes and blackbirds, chaffinches and sparrows, robins and starlings – just the common little birds of the countryside, and they were led by the blue Tom Tit, who had fetched his friends and neighbours to join the angels.

The Fir Tree shook his branches with amazement at the boldness and impudence of the birds, who had gone where no living creature dared to move in that heavenly host, but the Babe held out His little hands and called to them.

Then the birds sang their own carol of Christmas, so shrill and piping, with multitudinous whistlings and chirpings and twitterings, the noise of it drowned even the sweet song of the angels. But the Babe laughed and stroked the feathers of the blue Tom Tit, who was their leader, and the Tit swung from the altar rails and turned a somersault for the Child.

All this the Fir Tree saw as he stood in the starlit wood on Christmas Eve, and watched the Star of Bethlehem hanging over the old village church, and to me he told the story.

The Pixies' Scarf

ONCE upon a time there was an old woman who went out to pick whortleberries on Dartymoor. She carried a tin can in one hand and a basket in the other, and she meant to fill them both before she returned home.

Behind her came a little boy, her young grandson, Dicky, who had asked her to take him with her across the great windy moor. The old woman's eyes were on the ground, on the low green bushes which spread in a web for miles, but the little boy stared about him at the birds in the air, and the white clouds in the sky, and the great black tors like castles rising from the heather and grass.

'Grandmother, where does those birds come from?' he asked, but Mrs Bundle shook her head.

'Never mind the birds, Dicky. Pick the worts. There's lots of worts here. 'Tis blue with 'em,' and she stooped and gathered the little bloomy whortleberries with her gnarled old fingers, stripping them from the bushes, and dropping them into her can with a rattle like beads falling in a box.

So Dicky turned his head from the blue sky and the flittering birds, and looked at the rounded bushes, like dark-green cushions. Dartymoor was more full of lovely things even than the sky, he thought, as he bent down. He crammed his red mouth with berries, and put a handful in his own little basket. Then he knelt down to look at the scurrying beetles and ants and the long-legged spiders which hurried about their business in the green and scarlet leaves.

Suddenly his attention was caught by a wisp of rainbow colour, hanging on a twiggy branch of one of the bushes. He thought at first it was a spider's web, blue and green and gold, but when he picked it up he found it was woven silk, fine as the gossamer sacks which hang in the grasses, shimmering as the dewdrops in the grass.

'What have you got there?' asked old Mrs Bundle, as she saw him twist the rag round his finger and hold it up to the sun.

'It's a pretty something I've found,' said Dicky going up to her and showing the scrap of silk.

'Drop it, Dicky! Drop it! It's maybe something belonging to the Wee Folk.'

She lowered her voice to a whisper and looked round as if she expected to see somebody coming.

'It's a pixie-scarf you've found, I reckon,' she whispered. 'Put it back. It doesn't do to touch their things. They don't like it.'

She waited till he dropped the little scarf and then she went on gathering the berries, muttering to herself.

Dicky turned round and looked at the scarf. He couldn't

bear to leave it, so he whisked it up again, and slipped it in his pocket. Nobody would know, he told himself. He would take it home with him.

He wandered on, picking the ripe berries, following the old woman, staring and whistling, forgetting the little silken scarf, but as he ruffled the bushes with stained purple hands, and drew aside the tiny leaves, he was surprised to see far more things than he had ever imagined before. Down in the soil he saw the rabbits in their holes, playing and sleeping, or curled in their smooth dwelling houses. He saw the rocks and the little streams and trickles of water all flowing underground. Like a mirror was the ground and he watched the hidden life behind it. Many things were there, deep down, a rusty dagger, a broken sword blade, and he wandered on, staring at the secrets he discovered.

'Grandmother,' he called. 'See here. Here's something under the grass,' but the good old woman saw nothing at all except heather and whortleberries and the short sweet grass.

'Saints preserve us!' she cried, when Dicky scrabbled away the soil and brought up a broken crock of ancient coins. 'How did you know they were there?' she asked.

'I seed 'em,' said he.

She fingered the money and rubbed it on her torn skirt, but Dicky turned away. He didn't care about it. A new feeling had come to him, and he stood very still, listening, waiting.

The scent of the moor flowed to him, wild thyme and honey and moss in wet places. He could hear the countless bells of the purple heather ringing like merry church chimes, and the wind in the reeds sang like a harp, whilst the deep dark bogs sighed and moaned.

'I won't touch these,' said old Mrs Bundle, and she threw the coins away into the bog, but Dicky only laughed, for he heard new music as they fell and were sucked down to the depths. The earth itself seemed to be whispering, and the stream answered back, speaking to the bog and the emerald mosses.

'Get on with your picking,' scolded Mrs Bundle. 'You asked me to bring you with me a-worting, and here you are, finding queer things as ought to be hid. Whatever's took you, Dicky Bundle!'

But Dicky's eyes were wide with wonder, and he took no notice of his grandmother. Up in the trees were voices talking, two blackbirds were arguing, and he heard every word they said. A robin called: 'Come here! Take no notice of those people below. Come here!' and a tomtit swung on a bough and chattered to its friend, the linnet.

More than that, he could hear the low reedy voices of the worms in the stream's bank, and understand their language as they murmured on and on with placid talk of this and that, and pushed their way among the grasses.

Then came the shrill whisper of fishes in the water, and he leaned over the peaty stream to see who was there. Flat round eyes stared back at him, and the fishes swam under a rock as his shadow fell upon them. A kingfisher darted past, and Dicky heard its chuckle of glee as it dived and snatched up a weeping fish.

He would have stayed there all night, crouched on the stream's edge, hearkening to the talk of the creatures, listening to the music of the wild moorland, looking at the hidden life which was visible to his eyes, but his grandmother pulled his arm, and shook him.

'Didn't you hear me? Dick Bundle! Come away home. My basket and pail are full to the brim, but you've only got a tuthree! Shame on you for a lazy good-for-nothing little boy.'

Dicky was bewildered, and he followed her meekly along the road to the cottage down in Widdicombe, listening to voices all the way.

When they got home his grandmother emptied her fruit into the great brass pan, and soon there was a humming and bubbling as the jam simmered over the fire. Dicky took off his coat and hung it up behind the door, and when the scarf was away from him the little voices of mice in the wainscot and birds in the garden ceased. The cat purred, and he no longer knew what she said. The buzzing flies in the window lost their tiny excited little voices, the spider in the corner was dumb.

'It's gone very quiet,' said Dicky to his grandmother.

'Quiet? It's the same as usual. You go and fill the kettle and put it on ready for tea. Then wash your hands and face, for you are black as a nigger. No wonder you didn't find many berries! You ate 'em all!'

Mrs Bundle was indignant with her grandson, and when the two sat down to their tea she thought of her son, Dicky's father, away in America, earning his living far from the village he loved. She must bring Dicky up to be a good boy, worthy of that father. She sighed, and looked at her grandson, and shook her head wearily. It was hard for her with her old bones to have to deal with a lazy young sky-gazer like Dicky.

'Now you can go out and play,' she told Dicky when

the meal was finished and the table cleared. 'I shall make my jam ready for selling to customers, and maybe we shall get enough money to buy you a new pair of shoes, for you sadly need them.'

Dicky went out to Widdicombe Green and played at marbles with the other boys. Then Farmer Vinney let him take his brown mare to the stable, and Farmer Deacon asked him to catch a hen that had gone astray. So he was busy with this and with that, until the moon came up over the hills and the stars shone in the night sky, and the great tors disappeared in the shadows.

Then Dicky went indoors for his supper of bread and milk. He went upstairs to the little room with a crooked beam across the ceiling and he said his prayers and got into his wooden bed. Old Mrs Bundle came to look at him and tuck in the clothes.

'Now go to sleep, Dicky. I've brought your jacket upstairs, ready for morning. Go to sleep, and God bless you, my dear.'

But Dicky wasn't sleepy at all, and he lay with his eyes wide open staring at the moon over the moor and the tall tower of the church across the Green. After a time he heard a high silvery bell-like voice, calling and calling, so clear and fresh it was just as if the stars were speaking to one another.

'Dick Bundle! Dick Bundle!' cried the tiny voice. 'Give me back the scarf.'

'Dick Bundle! Dick Bundle!' echoed a hundred little voices, pealing like a chime of fairy bells, ringing like a field of harebells all swaying in the wind.

Dick sprang out of bed and looked through the window. In a rose-bush in the narrow garden below sat a little green man, holding a glow-worm in his hands, and Dicky knew he was a pixie. He saw the little creature's pointed cap, and his thin spindly legs, crossed as he squatted among the roses, and he caught the green glint of the pixie's eyes.

Behind were many more pixies, crowds of them, perched on the garden wall, clambering in the flower-beds, running across the grass, each one carrying a glow-worm and calling 'Dick Bundle' in its shrill tinkling voice.

'Give us back the scarf,' they sang.

'Come and fetch it,' called Dick Bundle through the window, and he went to his jacket pocket and took out the wisp of rainbow silk and held it dangling at the window.

How beautiful it looked! It was quite different with the moon shining upon it, and it moved like a shimmering fish, and glittered in his hands.

'Oh! Oh! Oh!' sang the pixies. 'There it is! There it is! Give it back!'

'Come and fetch it,' said Dicky again, for he wanted to try to catch one of the little men.

'We can't come in because you said your prayers,' they replied, and others echoed: 'Prayers. Prayers. No, we can't come in,' and their voices wailed and squeaked.

'You come down to us,' invited the first pixie, who seemed to be the leader. 'You bring it to us, Dick Bundle.'

'No,' replied Dick. 'I can't do that,' and he fondled the scarf and drew it through his fingers. 'I mustn't go out in the night, or I should catch rheumatics like my Grannie.'

He looked at his fingers and they were shining with

light where the scarf had touched them. Yes, it was too lovely a thing to lose!

'Throw it down to us, Dicky boy,' wheedled the nearest pixie. 'It belongs to our Queen, and she has been hunting for it all day.'

'How did you know it was here?' asked Dicky. 'I've never had it out of my pocket till now.'

'The birds and fishes and rabbits all knew you heard their voices, for you stopped to listen, and no human can understand what the other world says. Only the pixies know. So when they told us a boy had hearkened to their talk as they spoke to one another, and had found old coins lost under the ground, and had bent his head to listen to the heather bells and the gossamer harps in the bushes, then we knew you must have found the scarf. For it gives eyes and ears to those who are blind and deaf.'

'I'm not blind and deaf,' protested Dicky.

'Yes, you are. You can see nothing without the scarf. Throw it back to us, for you can't keep it. We shall torment you till we get it.'

'What will you give me for it?' asked Dicky.

'A carriage and pair,' said the pixie.

'Show it to me first,' said Dicky.

Then a tiny carriage rolled across the garden path, and it was made out of a cunningly carved walnut shell, drawn by a pair of field mice. The carriage was lined with green moss, and the coachman was a grasshopper with a whip of moonshine.

'I can't get into that,' Dicky complained. 'That's no good to me.'

He watched the little carriage bowl along into the shadows.

'What else will you give me?'

'A suit of armour,' suggested the pixie.

'Show me first,' said Dicky, and he leaned low, expecting to see a grand iron suit like the knights wore of old.

A little man staggered along the wall under the window, carrying a suit of shining armour, and the plates were made of fishes' scales, all blue and silver, and the helmet was adorned with a robin's feather.

'No. I couldn't wear that,' said Dicky. 'What else have you got?' He twisted the little scarf and waved it before the throng of agitated pixies, who wailed: 'Oh! Oh! Oh!' as they gazed at it, and held out their skinny arms for it.

'I'll give you a fine dress for your grandmother,' said the pixie. He brought out of the rose tree a little crinolined dress made of a hundred red rose petals.

'My grannie's too stout for that,' laughed Dicky. 'What else can you give me?'

The pixies scratched their heads with vexation. They didn't know what to give the great human boy who leaned from the window under the thatched roof. All their belongings were far too small for such a giant, they whispered to one another.

Then one of them had a thought. 'A bag of marbles,' said he.

Now Dicky was the champion marble player of Widdicombe-on-the-Moor, and he thought if he got some pixie marbles he might be the best player on the whole of Dartymoor.

Surely a pixie marble would capture every other, for there would be magic in it!

'Show them to me,' said Dicky, eagerly.

The little man dragged a brown sack up the wall, and emptied the marbles in a shining pile. Green as grass in April, blood-red, snow-white, and blue as the night-sky they shone, each one sparkling in the moonlight.

'Yes, I'll take the marbles, and you can have the scarf,' said Dicky. No boy at school had such pretty marbles, and if they were not quite round, and not as big as ordinary marbles, that did not matter.

He held out his hand for the sack, and dropped the scarf from the window, but he took care to grasp the sack before he let the scarf flutter down, for he had heard of the tricky ways of pixies, who outwit humans whenever it is possible. But they were so eager to get their precious scarf, they never even snatched at the bag. With excited happy cries, queer fluting songs and chuckles like a flock of starlings at evening, they clasped the scarf. Then singing, whistling, shouting, and waving their glow-worms, they ran away, and Dick could see the tiny lights disappear in the distance.

He put the little brown sack under his pillow, and crept into bed, for suddenly he was very tired and sleepy.

The next morning his grandmother aroused him, and he got ready for school.

'What have you got in that queer bag, Dicky?' asked Mrs Bundle, as Dicky stuffed it in his pocket. He brought it out reluctantly and showed it to her.

'Don't throw them away, Grannie. They're pixie marbles,' said Dick, frightened that he would lose his new possession.

'Pixie marbles? They are pixie rubies and emeralds and I don't know what!' cried his grandmother, holding up the glittering gems to the sunlight.

'You mustn't throw them away,' said Dicky sulkily. 'I am going to take them to school to play marbles.'

'These will buy all the marbles in the world, Dicky,' said Mrs Bundle. 'Now we shall be rich as rich. We will build a neat little house, and have an orchard, and keep a few cows and a horse or two.'

'And some pigs?' asked Dicky, quickly.

'Yes, pigs and hens and ducks, too. Yes, all of those and more beside. Perhaps we will have a donkey.'

'And a new pair of boots for me and a dress for you, Grannie?' asked Dicky.

'Yes, boots and a dress and a suit of good clothes, my child. Then I will write to your father and bring him home, for we must have him to help with the farm, mustn't we?'

'Yes, oh yes,' shouted Dicky, flinging his arms round her. 'And we'll live on Devonshire junket and cream, shall we, Grannie?'

'Maybe we will,' she replied. 'I think we can manage it.'

She trickled the jewels through her fingers, and tried to calculate their worth. Days of poverty were over, she could sit and rest in her old age, and help others, poor as herself. Yes, the pixies had brought fortune to her cottage.

But Dicky Bundle went running off, lest he should be late for school. In his pocket was one of the gems, a smooth, round, blood-red stone. It made a famous marble, and never missed its aim, so that Dicky became the champion player of all the boys on Dartymoor. That was more important than riches to him, and he took good care to tell nobody where his marble came from, lest it too should be sold, for money isn't everything.

Orion Hardy

Up in the hill country stands a little stone farmhouse I know very well, for I used to play hide-and-seek around the haystacks in the fenced stackyards, and I helped to drive up the cows from the long sloping fields which dip down to the valley.

It was a farm I liked very much because there was a romantic feeling about the place. It stood, sturdy and strong, with thick grey stone walls against the hill, and its smiling face peered down to the valley seven hundred feet below. At night it was like a lighthouse in the darkness, with one small light beaming from its windows.

I ran down the fields to that valley, down and down, as swiftly as the wind, till I came to the little brown brook at the bottom. I climbed the stiles and chased the squirrels in the woods, and scampered along the grassy track. Then, high above me, I could see one little attic window looking down at me from the farmhouse roof, and I waved my hand in good-bye.

The farm had had several owners who had left for one

thing and another. This was strange in a countryside where people stayed at their farms for a hundred years. It had the reputation of being unlucky. It was quite true that queer things happened there, but when I knew it the luck had come back and there was content. This is how it happened.

One day an old farm labourer walked up the fields with his bundle on his back and a stick in his hand. When he came to the gate of the farmyard he stood for a while leaning there, watching the house, and the house seemed to gaze back at him.

Then out came Farmer Holland, with his barking dogs at his heels. The dogs rushed forward and then wagged their tails and leapt joyously at the old man.

'What do you want? Have you lost your way?' asked the farmer.

'Have you work for me, Master?' asked the old man, and he opened the gate and walked slowly into the yard. 'I'm looking for a place, for I'm all alone now. I've been used to farming all my life, but I've been in London for a long time. I couldn't abide the pavements any more, so I've come back to the land where I belong.'

The farmer looked keenly at the hesitating old fellow, whose hands were trembling with excitement.

'Yes, I've plenty of work, plenty, but I doubt if you'd do for me. You're an old man, and it's a hard place here,' said Farmer Holland.

The old man's face drooped and his blue eyes dimmed with disappointment. Then little Tom Holland came running from the fields, hurrying to find out why the dogs had barked and the gate clicked. He stopped suddenly when he saw the stranger, but the old man crooked a finger and nodded to him in a friendly way, and Tom came forward and stood at his side.

The barn-door cock flew to the low wall of the grass-plat and crowed a welcoming 'Cock-a-doodle-doo!' A cuckoo called 'Cuckoo! Cuckoo!' from the walnut tree in the croft. The cat sidled from the stackyard and brushed the man's corduroys with her curling tail. A robin hopped near with inquisitive eye and then sang a cascade of music.

'Can you plough and sow? Can you reap and mow? Can you thatch a barn and mend a wall? Are you a bit of a vet, and can you look after horses?' asked the farmer, with a touch of scorn.

'Yes, Master, I can do all those things,' replied the old man simply, with no boasting.

'And you've not forgot, in London?' asked the farmer.

'We never forget,' said the old man, proudly.

'Well, I'll take you on till the harvest is over, and after that I'll make no promises. I'll see how you shape yourself.'

'Thank you, Master. Thank you. You won't regret it.' The old man spoke softly.

'See if you can earn your keep. It's hard to make a living here, what with one thing and another.'

'Yes, Master. Hard living doesn't daunt me. I'm used to it.'

'What's your name?' asked the farmer as he turned back to the house, with the old man following him.

'Orion Hardy, but they calls me Rion for short,' said the old man.

'Orion. Queer name. Name of stars. Come on in, Rion.'

'Orion,' murmured little Tom, and he took the old man's hand. 'Orion, I like you.'

'Here's Rion Hardy come to help us out, wife,' shouted Farmer Holland, throwing wide the door.

'I hope you can, for we need some helping,' said a quiet little voice, and Mrs Holland smiled at the old man and her Tom.

The old man went about the day's work, and at night he retired to the attic under the roof, with his bundle of clothes, and his stick in a corner. He looked through the window, down the long fields to the valley, and he began to whistle softly.

'Here I am, with a roof over my head, and a good supper inside me, and plenty of friends in the farmyard. I shan't do so badly,' said he, aloud.

'Badly,' echoed the room.

He started and looked around.

'I shall do well,' he said, firmly.

'Well?' asked the room.

'That's better,' said he.

'Better,' said the echoing voice.

He undressed and got into bed, but in the night he was wakened by an uneasy feeling. The bedclothes were twitched from over him, and the hard little pillow was pulled from under his head. A cold wind blew on his face, and there were rustlings. All his clothes, which he had left in a neat pile, were thrown about.

'Go to sleep, there,' he cried, and he could hear elfin laughter and the strange pattering of feet.

He said nothing when Mrs Holland asked him how he slept, except 'It was a bit company-like.'

Now he noticed that the house-place was untidy, the

cinders lay on the hearth, and milk was spilled on the floor. He helped to tidy it up, surprised by the mess.

'Seems as if the place is bewitched,' said Mrs Holland, sadly. 'Once I didn't believe in such things, but we have some queer goings-on. Things get lost and moved out of their places, as if somebody had a spite against us.'

'That's bad,' said Orion. 'Have you tried a branch of the wicken tree?' (The wicken tree is the rowan, which grows in hilly land.)

'Yes, I put boughs of the wicken tree over the doors, but it goes on just the same,' replied Mrs Holland.

Orion went out to the milking, and as he milked the cows he thought of the trouble at the farm and wondered what he could do. He fettled the mare and brushed up the stable, he suckled the calves and fed the pigs.

As he did the work, slowly and methodically, he forgot the farm's bad luck and the disturbances of the night in the pleasure he felt at being back with things he loved. He looked after the animals and opened the gates for them, with never a cross word when the cows blundered the wrong way, and he spoke gentle, soothing talk to the mare, and spoke to the pigs, encouraging them, as if they could understand him.

So the day went on, and little Tom Holland ran about with the new farm man, Orion, and helped him. But at night there was the same upset and disturbance, and Orion decided that he must leave the little room.

'I would like to change my bedroom if you don't mind, Missis,' he said, after he had put the attic to rights.

'We haven't another room, Rion. It's the same everywhere, worse in some than others,' said Mrs Holland.

'I'll sleep in the stable, Missis,' said Orion.

'Just as you like, Rion. Better folk than us have slept in stables, and perhaps you will find it more peaceful,' sighed the farmer's wife. 'I do wish we could get some quiet here.'

So the old man settled himself in the corner of the stable, with his bundle of clothes in the stone embrasure in the wall. He had a three-legged stool to sit on, and the mounting-block was his table. A heap of fresh golden straw, with a clean sack thrown over it, made a bed. That was all he wanted, and when the little yellow cat walked in to keep him company, and to kill the mice, he was delighted. The mare turned her head and watched him, and whinnied with joy to have him there.

Outside in the yard was the water-trough, cut out of an immense block of stone, and a spring ran into it with a singing trickle of fresh cold water. A bucket stood in the corner, and he swilled his face and dried it on his little towel. He combed his rough hair, and then he undressed by the light of a candle in the iron candlestick stuck in the wall.

Harness and bridle and bit hung from the stall, and horse brasses and martingale were fastened to the wooden beams of the roof. There was a fine horse blanket, striped red and yellow, to cover him, and his pillow was stuffed with sweet hay.

Just before he went to sleep he looked out of the door at the night sky and the stars. His own constellation, Orion, had gone, for it was early summer, but he could see the Great Bear and Cassiopeia's Chair. He could hear the water trickling into the trough, and it seemed to be saying something, but he could not catch the words. Across the yard the house was in darkness, except for the glimmer of a nightlight in little Tom's room.

'I'll make that whistle-pipe tonight, and give it him tomorrow,' said Orion. 'He's a nice little lad. He'll be right pleased to have it, and I'll play a tune to him.'

He took his clasp-knife and the piece of ash sapling he had brought with him from the fields, and by the light of the candle he cut the green bark and made the whistle-pipe.

Great shadows danced over the ceiling as he bent his head to the work, the mare turned to look at him, and the little cat rubbed against him.

'How's this, Jenny?' he asked, as he cut the last slit and made the small holes for the stops. 'Would you like a tune, lass?' He put the pipe to his lips and played an air, and the mare listened intently, flicking her ears with joy. Horses like music, especially the sound of soft notes from wooden pipes, and Jenny gave a snuffle of admiration as the old man played his tunes. Suddenly her ears went back and her eyes showed alarm. The cat's hair stood on end. A whispering shuffling sound came from the yard, and Orion went across to the door and opened the top half.

Over the cobbles pranced a host of grey shadows. They ran on tiptoe to the house and pressed close to the walls. They threw up their arms and leapt in the air.

'Them's the disturbers,' muttered Orion. 'Wouldn't I like to upset their pranks.'

He put his whistle-pipe to his mouth again and sent a stream of music swinging through the air, strange dancing music, which set the cat leaping and the mare nodding her great head. Then out from the house came the shadows, swaying and trembling in the moonlight, over the cobbles, and away through the gate.

Orion shut the stable door and got into his bed. He put his whistle-pipe under his pillow and fell fast asleep. Soon there was no sound but the soft purring of the little cat, the snores of Orion, and grunts of contentment from the mare.

The next day Orion went to the house for his breakfast. His milking was done, the mare fed, and the stable tidied. Mrs Holland was all smiles as she poured out his tea.

'No trouble last night, Orion,' said she. 'It's the first time for months. You must have brought us luck.'

'Did you make my whistle-pipe?' asked little Tom.

'Yes, Tom. Here it is. Yes, I made it last night, when the moon was shining, and it plays well. I'll play it when I've had my bit of summat to eat.'

Little Tom was delighted, and the old man played his tunes, and made even the cat dance again.

But Orion said nothing of the night's adventures, and he made another whistle-pipe to keep ready for the shadow-folk, if they should come again. Come they did, and he turned them away, whistling to them from the stable door, beguiling them from the farmhouse.

Other strange things happened at that farm on the hill. One day the farmer's wife called to Orion.

'Go and fetch some water, Rion. You'll have to carry it from the spring yonder in the fields. The water-trough here is dry.'

Sure enough, the singing trickle of cold water had disappeared, and there was not a drop to drink.

'What has happened to it, Ma'am?' asked the old man, as he slipped the yoke over his shoulders and fastened a pair of buckets to the chains.

'It dries up each year in summer, like this, and leaves us with never a drop.'

'It ought not to do that, Ma'am,' said Orion, and off he ambled across the fields with little Tom trotting by his side. As he went, he told the little boy all about water, running under the ground, and leaping up in a spring for people to drink.

'Where's our water gone?' asked Tom.

'Maybe it's got fast down there,' said Rion. He held the buckets to the trickle in the field from the silver spring that bubbled out of the ground.

'Listen,' cried Tom. 'There's somebody calling.'

'Set me free. Set me free,' sang a high, silvery voice, and Tom and Orion nodded and whispered.

'It's something down there,' said Tom.

When the buckets were full, Orion carried them back to the farm.

'That spring seems to be stopped up in the field,' said he. 'Shall I take a spade and clear it out?'

'Waste of time,' said Farmer Holland. 'It always was a poor spring. Don't bother over it.'

When evening came, after milking was over and there was some free time, the old man returned with a spade and dug a trench. He found that a great stone had stopped up the water. It came rushing out in a clear stream, gushing like a fountain, and a voice sang, 'I am free. I am free. I am free.'

Away ran the water, diving underground again; and when Orion got back to the farm, there was a rushing waterfall in the stone trough, to serve the house and farm.

That night, when Orion went to the stable to sleep, he could hear very distinctly the voice of the water talking and singing. It laughed as it fell on the stones to cool them, it chuckled with glee. When the band of shadows came out, as usual, they danced up to the spring instead of going to the house walls, and they all stooped and drank. Then deep into the earth they all sank, and were never seen again.

It was time to reap the corn, and every day was busy. The golden wheat was cut and bound into sheaves, and the sheaves were carried to the threshing floor of the great barn. Orion took his swingle and flail to thresh some corn to be ground into flour for the household.

As he worked there alone one day he heard a voice crying, 'Don't beat me. Don't beat me.'

He stopped and listened, but there was nobody to be seen. He swung his flail again, and again a voice cried out in piteous tones, 'Don't beat me.'

He turned over the corn, and there was a fine sheaf lying on the floor, with great golden ears, heavy as if they had been pure gold. He lifted it out and set it aside, for it was the pick of all the fields. He remembered it, wheat that had grown in a favoured spot, tall, red-gold wheat. The voice stopped, and he went on with the threshing.

The farmer came to the barn and picked up a handful of corn from the floor and let it run through his fingers. Then he noticed the fine sheaf set aside.

'Why have you left that? It's our best wheat. Get it threshed, Rion. I wanted to see its quality.'

'Nay, Master. I put it aside for the Harvest Thanksgiving. I'll make a good neat sheaf of it and take it to the church, for it's lovely corn.'

'I don't send anything there, Rion. It's good corn, and we need it.'

'Master, let me bind it afresh and take it down, for we've had a good harvest and we ought to give thanks.'

'Have it your own way, Rion,' said Farmer Holland, turning away. 'You always get your own way; and I will say this, things haven't been so bad lately.'

So Rion bound the sheaf with a twisted band of straw and carried it down to the church for the Harvest Festival. The vicar was much surprised, but he placed the golden sheaf right by the altar, as a thankoffering from the farm.

Little Tom went to church with his mother to see it on Sunday, but old Rion kept away.

'I'm not fine enough,' said he. 'I give my thanks to God in the stable and in the fields. That's where I belong.'

The harvest was over, and the old man prepared to go on his way. He was slower than ever, and he felt that the farmer would never keep him through the winter months when there was not much work to be done. So he packed his bundle one morning and came before the farmer.

'I'd best be going along,' said he. 'I've been happy here. I'll maybe come back for next harvest, if you want me.'

'You're not going, Rion?' asked Farmer Holland. 'You don't want to leave us, do you?'

'No, I don't want to go, but I thought as how . . .'

'Then stop. Say no more. Why, Rion, I do believe you've changed the luck of the farm. I don't know how you managed it, but it is different now,' said the farmer.

'Stay with us, Orion,' said Mrs Holland. 'You've brought us peace and contentment, and we've been happy with you.'

'Stay with us, Rion,' said little Tom. 'Nobody can make a whistle-pipe like you. Besides, you promised to make me a straw trumpet. You can't go.'

'And when winter comes you shall have the little attic, all made nice, for the house is quiet now,' added Mrs Holland.

So the old man stayed.

One day, when Rion was blowing his tuneful pipe of ash wood, Tom saw a host of golden people running from the fields. They danced over the gate and flew with short gold wings, like birds. Round the yard they went, leaping and laughing to the music. Old Rion could not see them, but Tom held his breath, lest they should disappear.

Jenny the mare saw them, and flicked her ears as she watched. The dogs and cat saw them, and lay gazing with content at the bright company. Then they seemed to fade away in the air, and Tom never saw them again.

'They are all about us,' Rion explained. 'We can't see them, but they are there. I expect they bring luck with them. They are happy and glad to be here, I know.'

So that is why I always looked back at the old farm, at the little attic window peering down the valley, at the strong walls and the great chimneys. I, too, was always looking for the golden host. The luck of the farm had changed, and little Tom became the farmer there, and then Tom's son followed after, but old Rion slept in the churchyard, with a sheaf of corn carved on his tombstone, and a whistle-pipe over it, so that people would never forget.

Sam Pig Seeks His Fortune

ONE day Sam Pig started out to seek his fortune, and this was the reason. He came down as usual for breakfast, with never a thought except that he was hungry and there was a larder full of food. It was a sunny morning and he decided he would bask in the garden, and enjoy himself, and do nothing at all.

'Go and fill the kettle at the spring,' said Ann, when he entered the room. He picked up the copper kettle and carried it down the lane to the spring of water which gushed out of the earth. Then he staggered slowly back, spilling all the way.

'That's my day's work done,' he said to himself as he lifted it to the fire.

'Go and chop some sticks, Sam,' said Bill, when he was comfortably settled at the table. He picked up the axe from the corner and went to the woodstack. Then he chipped and he chopped till he had a fine pile of kindling. He filled the wood-box and brought it back to the house.

'That's two days' work done,' said he to himself as he put some of the wood under the kettle. He returned to his seat but Ann called him again.

'Blow up the fire, Sam,' she ordered. He reached down the blow-bellows and he puffed and he huffed and he blew out his own fat cheeks as well as the bellows. Then the fire crackled and a spurt of flame roared out and the kettle began to sing.

'That's three days' work done,' said Sam to himself and he listened to the kettle's song, and tried to find out what it said.

'Go and fetch the eggs, Sam,' said Tom, and away he went once more. He chased the hens out of the garden and hunted under the hedgeside for the eggs. He put them in a rhubarb-leaf basket and walked slowly back to the house. His legs were tired already, and he looked very cross.

'That's four days' work done,' said he to himself, and he put the basket on the table. Then he sat down and waited for breakfast, but Ann called him once more.

'Sam. Wash your face and brush your hair,' she said. 'How can you sit down like a piggy-pig?'

That settled it! To be called a piggy-pig was the last straw! All Sam's plans suddenly changed. His life was going to be different. He had had enough of family rule.

'I'm going to seek my fortune,' he announced loudly, when he had scrubbed his face and hands and brushed his bristly hair. 'I'm going off right away after breakfast to seek my fortune.'

He put a handful of sugar in his cup and blew on his tea and supped his porridge noisily, in defiant mood.

'And what may that be?' asked Bill sarcastically. 'What is your fortune, Sam?'

'His face is his fortune,' said Tom rudely.

'You foolish young pig,' cried Ann. 'What would Badger say? You must stay at home and help us. We can't do without you.'

'I know you can't,' Sam tossed his head. 'That's why I'm going.' And he ate his breakfast greedily, for he didn't know when he would have another as good.

He took his knapsack from the wall and put in it a loaf of bread and a round cheese. He brushed his small hooves and stuck a feather in his hat. Then he cut a stick from the hazel tree and away he went.

'Good-bye,' he called, waving his hat to his astonished sister and brothers. 'Good-bye, I shall return rich and great some day.'

'Good-bye. You'll soon come running back, Brother Sam,' they laughed.

Now he hadn't gone far when he heard a mooing in some bushes.

'Moo! Moo! Moo!'

He turned aside and there was a poor lone cow caught by her horns, struggling to free herself. He unfastened the boughs and pulled the branches asunder so that the cow could get away.

'Thank you. Thank you,' said the cow. 'Where are you going so early, Sam Pig?'

'To seek my fortune,' said Sam.

'Then let me go with you,' said the cow. 'We shall be company.' So the cow and Sam went along together, the cow ambling slowly, eating as she walked, Sam Pig trying to hurry her.

'Take a lift on my back,' said the cow kindly, and Sam leapt up to her warm comfortable back. There he perched himself with his little legs astride and his tail curled up.

They went through woods and along lanes. Sam stared about from the cow's back, seeking his fortune everywhere.

'Miaou! Miaou!' The cry came from a tree, and Sam looked up in surprise. On a high bough sat a white cat, weeping and wailing in misery.

'What is the matter?' asked Sam.

'I've got up here,' sobbed the white cat, 'and I can't get down. I've been here for two nights and a day, and nobody has helped me. There's boogles and witches about in the night, and I'm scared out of my seven wits.'

'I'll get you down,' said Sam Pig proudly, and he stood on the cow's head and reached up with his hazel switch. The white cat slithered along it and slipped safely to the ground.

'Oh, thank you! Thank you, kind sir,' said the cat. 'I'll go with you, wherever you go,' said she.

'I'm going to seek my fortune,' said Sam.

'Then I'll go too,' said the white cat, and she walked behind the cow with her tail upright like a flag and her feet stepping delicately and finely.

Away they went to seek Sam's fortune, and they hadn't gone far when they heard a dog barking.

'Bow-wow. Bow-wow,' it said.

The cow turned aside and the cat followed, after a natural hesitation.

In a field they saw a poor thin dog with its foot caught in a trap. The cow forced the trap open and released the creature. Away it limped, holding up its paw, but Sam put a dock-leaf bandage upon it, and bound it with ribbons of grasses.

'I'll come with you,' said the dog gratefully. 'I'll follow you, kind sir.'

'I'm going to seek my fortune,' said Sam.

'Then I'll go too,' barked the dog, and it followed after. But the white cat changed her place and sprang between the cow's horns; and that's the way they went, the cow with Sam on her back and the cat between her horns and the lame dog trotting behind.

Now after a time they heard a squeaking and a squawking from the hedgeside. There was a little Jenny Wren, struggling for its life in a bird-net.

'What's the matter?' asked Sam.

'I'm caught in this net and if nobody rescues me, I shall die,' cried the trembling wren.

'I'll save you,' said Sam, and he tore open the meshes of the net and freed the little bird.

'Oh, thank you. Thank you,' said the wren. 'I'll go with you wherever you go.'

Then it saw the green eyes of the cat watching it from the cow's horns so it flew to the other end of the cow and perched on its tail. Away they all went, the cow with the pig on her back and the cat on her horns and the bird on her tail, and behind walked the dog.

They went along the woods and meadows, always seeking Sam's fortune. After a time it began to rain and they got bedraggled and wet. Then out came the sun and they saw a great rainbow stretching across the sky and dipping down to the field where they walked. The beautiful arch touched the earth at an old twisty hawthorn tree.

'That's where my fortune is hidden,' cried Sam, pointing to the thorn bush. 'At the foot of the rainbow. Badger told me once to look there. "Seek at the foot of a rainbow and you'll find a fortune," he said to me, and there's the rainbow pointing to the ground!'

So down they scrambled: the white cat leapt from the cow's horns, Sam sidled from the cow's back and the bird flew down from the cow's tail. They all began to dig and to rootle with horns and feet and bill and claws and snout. They tossed away the black earth and dug into the crumpled roots of the tree. There lay a crock filled with pieces of gold.

'Here's my fortune,' cried Sam Pig, lifting it out.

'We can't eat it,' said the cow, snuffing at it with her wet nose. 'It's hard as stone.'

'We can't eat it,' said the white cat, putting out a delicate pink tongue. 'It's tough as wood.'

'We can't eat it,' barked the dog, biting with sharp teeth at the gold. 'It's harsh as rocks.'

'We can't eat it,' sang the bird, pecking at the pieces. 'It's cruel as a snare.'

'What use is your fortune?' they all asked Sam.

'I don't know,' Sam shook his head and scratched himself behind the ear. 'I've found it, and that is what I set out to do.'

'I'm weary,' said the cow. 'Let us stay here all night.'

The cow began to crop the grass, and the cat supped the bowl of milk which the cow gave to it. The bird found a few fat worms where the earth had been disturbed. As for Sam, he shared his bread and cheese with the dog, and all were satisfied and at peace with one another. The cow tucked her legs under her big body and bowed her head in sleep. The cat curled up in a white ball.

The wren put its head under its wing. The dog rested with its chin on its paws.

Then Sam cut a stick from the hawthorn tree. It was a knobbly thorn full of magic, for it had guarded the gold for a thousand years, ever since the fairies had hidden it. Of course Sam didn't know that, but Badger would have warned him if he had been there.

'Never cut a bough from a twisty ancient thorn,' he would have said. 'There's a power of magic hidden in it.'

Sam cut the thorn and trimmed it with his clasp-knife, and leaned it up against the tree over the crock of gold, all ready to catch a robber if one should come in the night. Then he lay down next to the dog.

The moon came up in the sky and looked at the strange assembly under the old hawthorn tree. She blinked through the branches of the old thorn and shot her moonbeams at the cudgel, shaking it into life. Slowly it rose and staggered across the grass. Then it began to belabour every creature there except the little wren which was asleep in the tree.

When the cow felt the sharp blows across her ribs, she turned on the dog and tossed it with her sharp horns. The dog rushed at the cat and tried to worry it. The cat scrambled up the tree and tried to catch the bird. The little Jenny Wren awoke with a cry and flew away.

Sam took to his heels and ran as fast as he could along the lanes and through the woods and across the meadows till he reached home. He banged at the door and wakened them all up.

'Where's the fortune, Sam?' asked Bill and Tom and little Ann Pig. 'Did you find a crock of gold?'

'Yes. A crock of gold,' cried Sam, out of breath with running so fast. 'A crock of gold under the rainbow end.'

'Where is it?' they asked. 'Gold is useful sometimes and it would do fine to mend the hole in our roof. Where is it, Sam?'

Then Sam told how he had found the gold under the hawthorn tree, but the tree had belaboured them soundly in the night and he had run home.

'That gold is bewitched,' said Ann. 'Best leave it where you found it.'

'I would like to see the crock of gold, and touch it, and smell it,' interrupted Bill.

'So would I,' added Tom. 'I've never seen any gold.'

'Then I will take you there tomorrow after I've had a good sleep,' yawned Sam. 'That is if you don't make me work before breakfast.'

The next morning they all went across the wood and over the meadows to the old hawthorn tree where Sam had found the crock of gold.

A cow was feeding in the thick grass of the field, and a white cat was leaning with her paw outstretched over the stream fishing for minnows. A dog chased a rabbit through the hedge and a little Jenny Wren piped and sang.

There was no crock of gold anywhere to be seen, but underneath the old bent tree grew a host of king-cups, glittering like gold pence in the sunshine, fluttering their yellow petals in their dark green leaves.

'You imagined the gold,' said Bill indignantly. 'You've led us here on a wild-goose chase,' and he cuffed poor Sam Pig over the head.

'I didn't!' protested Sam. 'There's the cudgel I cut from the tree.'

On the ground lay a thick stick, knotted and thorny and dark. The pigs leaned over it without touching it; then they began to gather the flowers.

'Quite true,' they nodded. 'Quite true, Sam Pig. You did find a fortune after all. There it lies, all turned into yellow flowers, much more use than metal to a family of pigs. Let the human kind take the hard metal, and we'll take the posies. King-cups are good for pains and aches; their seeds make pills and their leaves are cool poultices and their flowers are a delight to our sharp noses.'

They gathered a bunch and walked slowly home through the fresh fields wet with dew. All the way they talked to Sam kindly and treated him as if he had indeed brought a fortune to them.

'Badger will be pleased with you, little Pigwiggin,' said they, and this was high praise for little Sam Pig.

The Easter Egg

ONE morning Susan looked out of her window and saw that spring had really come. She could smell it and she put her head far out, until she could touch the budding elm twigs. She pressed her hands on the rough stone of the window-sill to keep herself from falling as she took in deep draughts of the wine-filled air.

It was the elder; the sap was rushing up the pithy stems, the young leaves had pierced the buds, and now stuck out like green ears listening to the sounds of spring. The rich heady smell from the pale speckled branches came in waves, borne by soft winds, mixed with the pungent odour of young nettles and dock.

She wrinkled her nose with pleasure, and a rabbit with her little one directly below the window, on the steep slope, wrinkled her nose, too, as she sat up among the nettles and borage.

Susan laughed at the rabbit and ran downstairs. It was Good Friday and she had a holiday for a week.

Her mother met her in the hall, running excitedly to call her. There was a parcel addressed to Mr, Mrs, and Miss Garland. Susan had never been called Miss before, except by the old man at the village who said 'You're late, Missie,' when she ran past his cottage on the way to school.

With trembling fingers Susan untied the knots, for never, never had anyone at Windystone been so wasteful as to cut a piece of string.

Inside was a flower-embroidered tablecloth for her mother, a book of the Christian Saints and Martyrs of the Church for her father, which he took with wondering eyes, and a box containing six Easter eggs.

There were three chocolate eggs, covered with silver paper, a wooden egg painted with pictures round the edge, a red egg with a snake inside, and a beautiful pale blue velvet egg lined with golden starry paper. It was a dream. Never before had Susan seen anything so lovely. Only once had she ever seen an Easter egg (for such luxuries were not to be found in the shops at Broomy Vale), and then it had been associated with her disgrace.

Last Easter Mrs Garland had called at the vicarage with her missionary box and taken Susan with her. Mrs Stone had asked her to make some shirts for the heathen, and whilst they had gone in the sewing-room to look at the pattern, Susan, who had been sitting silent and shy on the edge of her chair, was left alone.

The room chattered to her; she sprang up, wide awake, and stared round. She had learnt quite a lot about the habits of the family from the table and chairs, when her eye unfortunately spied a fat chocolate egg, a bloated enormous egg, on a desk before the window. Round its stomach was tied a blue ribbon, like a sash.

Susan gazed in astonishment. What was it for? She put out a finger and stroked its glossy surface. Then she gave it a tiny press of encouragement, and, oh! her finger went through and left a little hole. The egg must have been soft with the sunshine. But who would have thought it was hollow, a sham?

She ran and sat down again, deliberating whether to say something at once or to wait till she was alone with her mother. Mrs Stone returned with Mrs Garland saying, 'Yes, Mrs Stone, of course I won't forget the gussets. The heathen jump about a good deal, they will need plenty of room.' But before Susan could speak, a long-haired, beaky-nosed girl ran into the room, stared at Susan and went straight to the Easter egg.

'Who's been touching *my* Easter egg?' she cried, just like the three bears.

They all looked at Susan and with deep blushes she whispered, 'I did.'

They all talked at once, Mrs Garland was full of apologies and shame, Mrs Stone said it didn't matter, but of course you could see it did, and the bear rumbled and growled.

When she got home Susan had to kneel down at once and say a prayer of forgiveness, although it was the middle of the morning. 'You know, Susan, it's very wrong to touch what isn't yours.'

But this perfect blue egg! There was never one like it. She put it in her little drawer in the table where her treasures were kept, the book of pressed flowers, the book of texts in the shape of a bunch of violets, the velvet

Christmas card with the silk fringe, and the card that came this Christmas.

Tenderly she touched them all. In the egg she placed her ring with the red stone, and a drop of quicksilver which had come from the barometer. She closed the drawer and went off to tell anyone who would listen – the trees, the dog, the horses.

But what a tale to tell the girls at school! She wouldn't take it there or it might get hurt, a rough boy might snatch it from her, or the teacher might see her with it and put it in her desk.

'Mother, may I ask someone to tea to see my egg?' she asked, fearing in her heart that no one would come so far.

'Yes, my dear,' and Mrs Garland smiled at her enthusiasm, 'ask whoever you like.'

She hurried through the woods and along the lanes to school, saying to herself. 'Do you know what I had at Easter? No. Guess what I had at Easter. No. My godmother, who is a real lady, sent me such a lovely Easter present. It was a box of eggs, and one was made of sky-blue velvet and lined with golden stars.'

At break the children walked orderly to the door and then flung themselves out into the playground, to jump and 'twizzle', hop and skip, to dig in their gardens, or play hide-and-seek.

Susan had a circle of girls round her listening to the tale of the egg. They strolled under the chestnut trees with their arms round each other.

'It's blue velvet, sky-blue, and inside it is lined with paper covered with gold stars. It's the most beautiful egg I ever saw.' The girls opened their eyes and shook their curls in amazement.

'Bring it to school for us to see,' said Anne Frost, her friend.

'I daren't, Mother wouldn't let me, but you can come to tea and see it.'

'Can I?' asked one. 'Can I?' asked another.

Susan felt like a queen and invited them all. Big girls came to her, and she invited them. The rumour spread that Susan Garland was having a lot of girls to tea. Tiny little girls ran up and she said they might come too. She didn't know where to draw the line, and in the end the whole school of girls invited themselves.

They ran home at dinner-time to say that Susan Garland was having a party, and they were brushed and washed and put into clean pinafores and frocks, with blue necklaces and Sunday hair-ribbons.

Susan sat on a low stone wall eating her sandwiches, excited and happy. She was sure they would all be welcome and she looked forward to the company in the Dark Wood.

After school she started off with a crowd of fifty girls, holding each other's hands, arms entwined round Susan's waist, all pressed up close to her. They filled the narrow road like a migration, or the Israelites leaving the bondage of Egypt.

Mothers came to their doors to see them pass, and waved their hands to their little daughters. 'Those Garlands must have plenty of money,' said they.

Susan was filled with pride to show her beautiful home, the fields and buildings, the haystacks, the bull, and her kind mother and father and Becky and Joshua who would receive them.

They went noisily through the wood, chattering and

gay, astonished at the long journey and the darkness of the trees, clinging to one another on the little path lest an adder or fox should come out, giggling and pushing each other into the leaves. The squirrels looked down in wonder, and all ghostly things fled.

Mrs Garland happened to stand on the bank that day to watch for Susan's appearance at the end of the wood; she always felt slightly anxious if the child were late.

She could scarcely believe her eyes. There was Susan in her grey cape and the new scarlet tam-o'-shanter, but with her came a swarm of children. She had forgotten all about the vague invitation.

Was the child bringing the whole school home?

She ran back to the house and called Becky and Joshua. They stood dumbfounded, looking across the fields.

'We shall have to give them all something to eat coming all that way,' she groaned.

'It will be like feeding the five thousand in the Bible,' exclaimed Becky, and Joshua stood gaping. He had never known such a thing. What had come over the little maid to ask such a rabble?

'What will her father say?' was everyone's thought.

They went to the kitchen and dairy to take stock. There was Becky's new batch of bread, the great earthenware-crock full to the brim, standing on the larder floor. There was a dish of butter ready for the shops, and baskets of eggs counted out, eighteen a shilling. There was a tin of brandy snaps, to last for months, some enormous jam pasties, besides three plum cakes.

They set to work, cutting and spreading on the big table, filling bread and butter plates with thick slices.

Joshua filled the copper kettles and put them on the

fire, and counted out four dozen eggs, which he put on to boil. 'We can boil more when we've counted the lasses.'

Roger the dog nearly went crazy when he saw the tribe come straggling and tired up the path to the front of the house. Susan left them resting on the wall and went in to her mother.

'I've brought some girls to tea, Mother,' she said, opening her eyes at the preparations.

'Oh, indeed,' said Mrs Garland. 'How many have you brought?'

'A lot,' answered Susan. 'Where's my egg, they want to see it?'

'Susan Garland,' said Mrs Garland severely, taking her by the shoulders, 'whatever do you mean by bringing all those girls home with you? Don't talk about that egg. Don't you see that they must all be fed? We can't let them come all this way without a good tea. You mustn't think of the egg, you will have to help.'

Susan looked aghast, she realized what she had done and began to cry.

'Never mind, dry your eyes at once and smile. I don't know what your father will say, but we will try to get them fed before he comes.'

Mrs Garland began to enjoy herself, she was a born hostess and here was a chance to exercise her hospitality.

She went out to the children and invited them to have a wash at the back door, where she had put a pancheon of hot water and towels. Then they were to sit orderly on the low walls, along the front of the house, and wait for tea which would come out in a few minutes. She chose four girls to help carry the things, and then she returned, leaving smiles and anticipation.

The fifty trooped round the house and washed their hands and faces, with laughter and glee. They peeped at the troughs, and admired the pig-cotes, but Susan shepherded them back to the walls where they sat in their white pinafores like swallows ready for flight.

Becky and Joshua carried out the great copper tea-urn, which was used at farm suppers and sometimes lent for church parties. Mrs Garland collected every cup and mug, basin and bowl in the house, from the capacious kitchen cupboards and tall-boy, the parlour cupboards, the shelves, the dressers, from corner cupboards upstairs, from china cabinet stand, and what-not, from brackets and pedestals.

There were Jubilee mugs, and gold lustre mugs, an old china mug with 'Susan Garland, 1840' on it, and several with 'A present for a Good Girl'. There were mugs with views and mugs with wreaths of pink and blue flowers, with mottoes and proverbs, with old men in high hats and women in wide skirts. There were tin mugs which belonged to the Irishmen, and Sheffield plated mugs from the mantelpiece, pewter and earthenware. There were delicate cups of lovely china, decorated with flowers and birds, blue Wedgwood, and some Spode breakfast cups, besides little basins and fluted bowls.

Becky poured out the tea, and Susan took it to each girl, with new milk and brown sugar. Old Joshua, wearing an apron, walked along the rows with a clothes-basket of bread and butter and a basket of eggs. As soon as he got to the end he began again.

Mrs Garland took over the tea, and sent Becky to cut more and more. Susan's legs ached and an immense hunger seized her, she had eaten nothing but sandwiches since her breakfast at half past seven. But there was no time, the girls clamoured for more, and she ran backwards and forwards with her four helpers, who had their own tea in between.

A clothes-basket was filled with cut-up pieces of cake, pastry, slabs of the men's cake, apple pasty, and currant slices. Then the box of ginger-snaps was taken round, and some girls actually refused. The end was approaching, but still Joshua walked up and down the line with food.

Dan came from out of the cow-houses with the milk, and Mr Garland followed. Nobody had been in the smaller cow-houses. What was Joshua doing in an apron, and Becky too when she should be milking?

He stared at the rows of chattering children and walked in the house. Mrs Garland ran to explain.

'Don't be cross with her,' she said.

He said nothing till Susan came in for more cake.

Then he stood up and looked at her, and Susan quailed.

'Dang my buttons, Susan Garland, if you are not the most silly soft lass I ever knew! Are you clean daft crazy to bring all that crowd of cackling childer here?'

Then he stamped out to the byres and Susan walked back with her slices of cake, thankful she had not been sent to bed.

At last the feast was finished and Becky and Mrs Garland washed up the cups and mugs, and collected the egg-shells, whilst Joshua went milking, and Susan ran for a ball to give them a game in the field before they went home. They ran races, and played hide-and-seek and lerky, they played ticky-ticky-touch-stone round the great menhir, and swarmed over its surface.

At the end of an hour Mrs Garland rang a bell and they came racing to her. 'Put on your coats now, my dears, and go home, your mothers will expect you, and you have a long walk before you.'

So they said good-bye, and ran off singing and happy, down the hill. Two little girls had come shyly up to Susan with a parcel before they went.

'Mother said if it was your birthday we were to give you this,' and they held out a ball like a pineapple. But Susan had to confess it wasn't her birthday and they took it home.

She went indoors and sat down, tired and famished, at the table. 'And, Mother, I never showed them my sky-blue egg after all! But they did enjoy themselves.'

Mrs Mimble and Mr Bumble Bee

In nearly the smallest house in the world lived Mrs Mimble, a brown field mouse. She had bright peeping eyes and soft silky reddish hair, which she brushed and combed each morning when she got out of bed. She was a widow, for her husband went to market one night for some corn, and never returned. Old Mr Toad said he had met Wise Owl on the way. This made Mrs Mimble nervous, and a loud sound would startle her so much she would lock her door and go to bed.

There was only one room in the nearly-smallest house, and that was the kitchen. Here Mrs Mimble did her cooking and sewing, but on wash-day she rubbed her linen in the dew and spread it out on the violet leaves to dry. In a corner of the kitchen was a bed, and above it ticked a dandelion clock. In another corner was a wardrobe, and there hung her best red dress edged with fur, and her bonnet and shawl, and the white bow she wore on her breast.

The house was built under a hedge, among the leaves. Its chimney reached the bottom bell of the tall foxglove, which overshadowed the little dwelling like a great purple tree. Mrs Mimble could put her head out of the kitchen window and listen to the bees' orchestra in the mottled flowers. She dearly loved a tune, and she hummed to the bees as she went about her work. Her house was so cleverly hidden, no one would notice it. Even the tiny spiral of smoke from her chimney disappeared among the foxglove leaves like blue mist, and left only the smell of woodruff in the air.

Farther on, separated from her home by a wild rose-bush, was the very smallest house in the world.

There lived Mr Bumble Bee. He also had only one room, but it was so little, and so crowded with furniture, it was lucky he could fly, for he never could have walked through his very little door at the end of the passage.

Mr Bumble was a stout furry bee, with such a big voice that when he talked his pots rattled, and the little copper warming-pan which hung on the wall often fell down with a clatter. So he usually whispered indoors, and sang loudly when he was out in the open where nothing could be blown down. The trees and bushes were too firmly rooted for that.

He was a merry old bachelor, and it was quite natural that he and gentle Mrs Mimble should be great friends.

All through the winter the little neighbours were very quiet. Mr Bumble Bee felt so drowsy he seldom left his bed. He curled himself up in the blankets, pulled the bracken quilt over his head, and slept. His fire went out, but the door was tightly shut, and he was quite warm. Now and then he awoke and stretched his arms and legs.

He fetched a little honey from his store of honey-pots in the passage and had a good meal. He drank a cup of honey-dew, and then got back to bed again.

Mrs Mimble was asleep in her house, too. The wind howled and gusts of hail beat against the door. Snow covered the ground with its deep white eiderdown, and Mrs Mimble opened her eyes to look at the unexpected brightness at the small window. She jumped out of bed and had a dinner of wheaten bread from the cupboard; but the cold made her shiver, and she crept back under her blankets and brown silk quilt.

Sometimes, when she felt restless, she sat in her chair, rocking, rocking, to the scream of the north wind. Sometimes she opened the door and went out to look for holly berries and seeds, but she never stayed long. Sometimes she pattered to the Bumble Bee's house, but the smallest house in the world was tightly shut, and she returned to bed for another sleep. No smoke came from the neighbouring chimneys; there were no busy marketings in the wood and orchard, no friendly gossips on the walls. All the very wee folk, the butterflies, bees, and ants, were resting.

One morning a bright shaft of sunlight shone straight through the window on to the mouse's bed, and a powder of hazel pollen blew under the door and settled on Mrs Mimble's nose. She sneezed, Atishoo! and sprang up.

'Whatever time is it? Have I overslept? Catkin and pussy willow out, and I in bed?'

She washed her face in the walnut basin, and brushed her glossy hair. Then she put on her brown dress with the fur cuffs, and pinned a white ribbon to her breast.

'I must pop out and look at the world,' said she to herself. 'Are the snowdrops over, I wonder?'

She reached down her bonnet and shawl, opened wide her window, and set off.

Mr Bumble's door was fast shut, and although she knocked until her knuckles were sore, no sound came from the smallest house, and no smoke came from the chimney.

The sun shone down and warmed Mrs Mimble's back, and she laughed as she ran up the hill.

'Soon he will wake, and won't I tease him!' she chuckled.

She crept under a tall narrow gate into the orchard on the hillside. Over the wall hung clusters of white rock, heavy with scent, and among the flowers sang a chorus of honey-bees.

'Bumble is getting lazy,' said Mrs Mimble. 'He ought to be up and out now,' but the bees took no notice. They were far too busy collecting honey for their hive in a corner of the orchard to listen to a field mouse.

Under the wall was a bed of snowdrops. They pushed up their green spear-like leaves and held the white drops in veils of green gauze. Mrs Mimble wrinkled her small nose as she ran from one to another, sniffing the piercingly sweet smell of spring. In a corner a company of flowers was out, wearing white petticoats and green embroidered bodices. Mrs Mimble sat up on her hind legs and put out a paw to stroke them. The bells shook at her gentle touch, and rang a peal, 'Ting-a-ling-spring-a-ling'.

She turned aside and ran up the high wall to the white rock and gathered a bunch for Mr Bumble Bee, to the honey-bee's annoyance.

'Let him get it himself,' they grumbled.

Then down she jumped, from stone to stone, and hunted for coltsfoot in the orchard to make herb-beer.

Time had slipped away, and the sun was high when she neared home. A fine smoke, which only her sharp eyes could spy, came from Mr Bumble's chimney. The door was wide open, and a crackly sound and a loud Hum-m-m-m came from within as the Bumble Bee cleaned his boots and chopped the sticks.

There was no doubt Mr Bumble was very wide awake, but whether it was through Mrs Mimble knocking at the door, or spring rapping at the window, nobody knows.

As Mrs Mimble stood hesitating, a three-legged stool, an arm-chair, and a bed came hurtling through the air and fell on the gorse-bush over the way.

'There it goes! Away it goes! And that! And that!' shouted Mr Bumble, and the warming-pan and the kettle followed after.

'Whatever are you doing, Mr Bumble?' exclaimed Mrs Mimble, now thoroughly alarmed.

'Oh, good day, Mrs Mimble. A Happy New Year to you,' said the Bee, popping a whisker round the door. 'I'm spring-cleaning. There isn't room to stir in this house until I've emptied it. I am giving it a good turn-out,' and a saucepan and fiddle flew over the mouse's head.

'It's a fine day for your spring-cleaning,' called Mrs Mimble, trying to make her high little squeak heard over the Buzz-Buzz, Hum, Hum, Hum-m-m, and the clatter of dishes and furniture.

'Yes, Buzz! Buzz! It is a fine day. I think I slept too long, so I'm making up for lost time.'

'Lost thyme, did you say? It isn't out yet, but white rock is, and I have brought you some.' She laid her bunch near his door.

But when a table crashed down on her long slender tail, she fled past the gorse-bush where the bed lay among the prickles, past the rose-bush where the fiddle and warming-pan hung on the thorns, to her own little house. She pushed open the door and sank on a chair.

'Well, I never!' she cried. 'I'm thankful to get safely here, and more than thankful that rose-bush is between my house and Mr Bumble's! His may be the tiniest house in all the world, it is certainly the noisiest!'

She looked round her kitchen, and for the first time noticed a cobweb hanging from the ceiling, and drifted leaves and soil on her grass-woven carpet.

Up she jumped and seized a broom. Soon she was as busy as Mr Bumble. She hung out the carpet on a low branch of the rose tree to blow in the wind and she scrubbed her floor. She swept the walls, and hung fresh white curtains at the window, where they fluttered like flower-petals. She festooned her blankets on the bushes, and wound up the dandelion clock, and polished her table and chairs. She made the teapot shine like a moon-beam.

All the time she could hear a loud Hum-Hum-Boom-Boom-Buzz coming from over the rose-bush, and a bang and clatter as knives, forks, and spoons flew about.

When she had finished her work, and her house smelled of wild-thyme soap and lavender polish, Bumble Bee was collecting his possessions from the gorse-bush and rose-bush where they had fallen.

'Boom! Boom! Buzz! Help me, Mrs Mimble!' he

called, and she ran outside and sat with little paws held up, and her bright eyes inquiring what was the matter.

'I've lost a spoon, my honey-spoon. It has a patent handle to keep it from falling in the honey-pot, and now I've lost it,' and he buzzed up and down impatiently, seeking among the spiny branches of the rose-bush.

Mrs Mimble looked among the brown leaves of the foxglove, but it wasn't there. She turned over the violet leaves, and peeped among the green flowers of the Jack-by-the-hedge, and ran in and out of the gorse-bush, but still she could not find it.

It was lost, and Mr Bumble grumbled so loudly that a passer-by exclaimed: 'It is really spring! Listen to the bees humming!'

Except for the loss of his spoon Mr Bumble was perfectly happy, and his friend, Mrs Mimble, was so merry it was a joy to be near her. Although she was too large to enter his house, he used to visit hers, and many an evening they spent before her open window, eating honey and wheat biscuits, and sipping nectar as they listened to the song of the bees. Each day was a delight to these little field-people.

One morning the Mouse knocked on Mr Bumble's door and called to him to come out.

'I have some news, Mr Bumble, some news! I've found a nest to let,' she cried.

Mr Bumble was resting after a long flight across the Ten-Acre Field, but he put down his newspaper and flew to the door.

'A nest? What do you want with a nest?' he asked.

'It's a chaffinch's nest, a beautiful old one, lined with

the very best hair and wool. It will make a summer-house, where I can go for a change of air now and then.'

'Shall we both go and see it?' asked the Bee, kindly.

Mrs Mimble ran home and put on her best red dress with fur edging, and her brown bonnet and shawl in honour of the occasion. The Bee combed his hair and brushed his coat with the little comb and brush he carried in his trousers pocket.

They walked down the lane together, but soon Mr Bumble was left behind. He was such a slow walker, and Mrs Mimble was so nimble, she ran backwards and forwards in her excitement, urging him on.

'Come on, Mr Bumble. Hurry up, Mr Bee,' she cried.

'It's this dust that gets on my fur,' said the Bee. 'Besides, you must remember that my legs are shorter than yours.'

He puffed and panted and scurried along, but Mrs Mimble was impatient.

'Can't you fly?' she asked.

'Oh, yes, I can fly,' he replied, ruffled because he wished to try to walk with her. He shook the dust from his legs, and with a deep Hum-m-m-m he soared up into the air. Higher and higher he flew, into the branches of the beech tree, where he buzzed among the long golden buds with their tips of green.

'Now he's gone, and I have offended him,' said the Mouse ruefully. She sat sadly on a daisy tuffet, with her tearful eyes searching among the trees for her friend. At length she spied him, swinging on a twig, fluttering like a goldfinch on a thistle.

'Come down, Mr Bumble, come down,' she piped in her wee shrill voice. 'I will run, and you shall fly just over my head, then we shall arrive together. And I do think you are a splendid pedestrian for your size.'

Mrs Mimble looked so pathetic and small down there under the great trees, that he relented and flew down to her. He was flattered too at the long word she had used. So they travelled, great friends again, along the lane, under the hedge of thorn and ash, she running in and out of the golden celandines and green fountains of Jack-by-the-hedge, he buzzing and singing and sipping the honey as he flew near.

When they reached the thickest part of the hedge, she ran up a stout hawthorn bush, and leaped into a small oval nest which had a label 'To Let' nailed to it by a large thorn.

'Isn't it a perfect house, with a view, too!' said the Mouse, waving her paw to the hills far away.

The Bee perched near on a bough, and swayed backwards and forwards with admiration. The nest was green and silver with moss and lichen, delicate as a mistletoe bunch. Its roof was open to the stars, but an overhanging mat of twigs and leaves kept out the rain. All that Mrs Mimble needed was a coverlet, and then she could sleep, lulled by the wind.

'I shall bring my brown silk quilt and keep it here, for no one will take it, it's just like a dead leaf. When I want a change of air, I shall come for a day or two, and live among the May blossom.'

They agreed she should take possession at once.

Mr Bumble, whose handwriting was neat, wrote another notice, and pinned it to the tree, for all to read who could.

MRS MIMBLE
HER HOUSE
PRIVATE

The very next day she came with the brown silk quilt, and her toothbrush and comb packed in a little bag. The Bee sat outside his own small house, and waved a red handkerchief to her.

'Good-bye. I will keep the robbers from your home,' he called, and he locked her door and put the key in his pocket.

Mrs Mimble climbed up to her summer-house, and leaned from the balcony to watch the life below.

Ants scurried along the grass, dragging loads of wood for their stockades. Sometimes two or three carried a twig, or a bundle of sticks. One little ant dropped his log down a hole, and all his efforts could not move it. As he pulled and tugged a large ant came up and boxed his ears for carelessness. Then he seized the wood and took it away himself to the Ant Town.

'A shame! A shame!' called Mrs Mimble. 'It's the little fellow's log. He found it,' but no one took any notice, and the small weeping ant dried his tears on the leaves.

Then Mrs Mimble heard a tinkle of small voices, and a ladybird came by with her five children dressed in red spotted cloaks.

'How many legs has a caterpillar got, Mother?' inquired a tiny voice, but the mother hurried along, and then flew up in the air with the children following, and Mrs Mimble, who nearly fell out of her nest as she watched them, never heard the answer.

'I will ask Mr Bumble,' said she. 'He knows everything.'

Two beetles swaggered up and began to fight. They rose on their hind legs and cuffed and kicked each other. They circled round and round one another, with clenched fists and glaring eyes.

'It's mine. I found it,' said one beetle, swinging out his arm.

'Take that, and that!' shouted the other, boxing with both arms at once, and dancing with rage. 'I saw it fall, and I had it first.'

'I carried it here,' said the first beetle, parrying the blows.

Mrs Mimble glanced round, and there, on a wide-open dandelion, lay a tiny gleaming spoon – Bumble Bee's honey-spoon with the patent handle.

Softly she ran down the tree, and silently she slipped under the shelter of the jagged dandelion leaves, and put the spoon in her pocket. Then she returned as quietly as she had come, and still the beetles banged and biffed each other, shouting, 'It's mine.'

At last, tired out, they sat down for a minute's rest, and lo! the treasure was gone! Whereupon they scurried here and there, hunting in the grass, till Mrs Mimble lost sight of them.

She put on her bonnet, intending to run home with the find, when she heard the loud Zoom! Buzz! Buzz! of her friend, and the Bumble Bee came blundering along in a zig-zag path, struggling to carry a long bright object on his back.

'I thought the new house might be damp,' he panted, bringing the copper warming-pan from across his wing, 'for no one has slept in it since the chaffinches were here last spring.'

'Oh, Mr Bumble, how kind you are! How thoughtful!' exclaimed the Mouse. She rubbed the warming-pan, which contained an imprisoned sunbeam, over the downy nest and drove out the little damps.

'Now I have something for you,' she continued, and she took from her pocket the honey-spoon, the small spoon as big as a daisy petal with its patent handle and all.

The sun came out from behind a round cloud, the small leaves packed in their sheaths moved and struggled to get out. Mrs Mimble heard the sound of the million buds around her, whispering, uncurling, and flinging away their wraps as they peeped at the sun. She leaned from her balcony and watched the crowds of field creatures, snails and ants, coming and going in the grassy streets below.

But restless Mr Bumble flew away for his fiddle, away across the field and along the lane to his own smallest house. He tuned the little fiddle, and dusted it, and held it under his wide chin. Then he settled himself on a bough near his dear friend, and played the song of the Fairy Etain, who was changed into a bee, in Ireland, a thousand years ago, but has always been remembered in legend and verse by the bees themselves.

The gentle Mouse sat listening to his tiny notes, sweet as honey, golden as the sunlight overhead, and she was glad, for she knew that summer was not far away.

The Besom Tree

THE smoke rose in a blue spiral from the cottage chimney. It floated up higher and higher till it was lost in the leaves of the crab-apple tree. Sam Pig lay on his back staring up at it, as it curled and waved like a flag. Sister Ann was putting another log on the fire, for a shower of sparks blew out, and a thicker wave of smoke arose.

'Somebody's cooking something,' Sam told himself. 'Ann's maybe making a roly-poly pudding or a savoury duffy for me to eat later on.' He popped a humbug into his mouth, and slowly roused himself and stretched his short legs. Round the corner of the garden he could see Bill working at the potato patch, and Tom was chopping wood. Then the house door opened and a cloud of dust flew out. Ann was sweeping with a little birch brush.

'If I keep still she won't see me,' thought Sam, and he dropped and lay motionless. 'She'll think it's the shadow of a pig lying here.'

'Sam! Sam!' called Ann, but he held his breath and kept his eyes shut.

'Silly Sam. I can see you,' mocked Ann, and she pushed the bristly brush in his face. 'Go and fetch some twigs from the silver birch tree. My besom is worn away.'

'How'll I get them?' Sam yawned and dragged himself up. 'How'll I know a silver birch tree, Ann?'

'It's a tree with besoms on it of course,' said Ann, laughing. 'There are lots of silver birches in the woods. Take your clasp-knife and cut the twigs and bind them into a besom. Quick, Sam! Off you go!'

Sam hitched up his trousers, scratched his head and put his hand in his pocket to feel the sharp blade of the knife. He strolled over to his brothers, but they went on digging and chopping as if he were not there.

'I'm going to find a silver birch tree,' confided Sam. 'How shall I know which it is? Besoms grow on it, Ann says.'

Tom and Bill looked up at their young brother Pig.

'It's not an oak tree with good-tasting acorns growing on it. It's not an elm tree with flat green pennies growing on it. It's not a sycamore with double keys growing on it,' said Tom solemnly.

'It's not a crab tree with little green apples, nor a wild cherry with bunches of flowers on its boughs. It's not a holly tree prickly as a hedgehog, nor a hawthorn with good-tasting haws,' said Bill, and he stopped digging and stood with his foot on the spade, thinking deeply.

Sam was very much interested, and he repeated after them, 'It's not an oak tree, nor an elm tree. It's not a crab nor a wild cherry.' Then he inquired, rather anxiously, 'What is it, if it isn't these?'

'A silver birch tree,' said Bill, and Tom added, 'Of course, a silver birch tree. Silver, you know, and birch for besoms.'

'Silver like the shillings Man got for my acting when he stole me,' murmured Sam, 'and birch like the besom Ann uses to sweep the floor.'

'Yes. Clever Sam. That's exactly it,' they agreed. 'Now get you gone and find it.'

Sam ran off down the lane towards the great green wood, where wolves and bears would live if Badger let them. Badger was somewhere in the depths, but nobody had seen him. He hadn't been home since before Christmas, and Sam wished the bulky shape of his friend would steal silently out of the shadows. There were perky rabbits, and cheeky squirrels, and a wicked-looking stoat, but never a good honest badger among them.

It was a fine afternoon and the birds were singing so loudly Sam raised his own squeaky voice to drown their clamour. It was just the day to find things – birds' nests, butterflies, bachelors' buttons, brandy-balls – anything beginning with a B, except a birch tree. Sam scrambled through the stile and entered the green glade of the wood. There was a narrow mossy path under the trees, pushing under hollies and skirting the oaks. Sam recognized it as the wood-creatures' own path and he trotted along it. Bees hummed around him, drinking the honey from the flowers in a clearing, sipping the sweetness from the great limes overhead. He stood still and considered them. They sipped and then rose in the air to fly towards a hollow tree.

Sam ran after them to the old tree and stared at the hole where the bees were coming and going.

'It's not a cherry tree with bunches of flowers on its boughs or a hawthorn with good-tasting haws. It's not an oak with acorns or a sycamore with double keys, or a birch with besoms,' said Sam to himself. 'It's a honey tree, with honeycomb inside it. That's what it is.'

'A piece of honeycomb from the honey tree would be much better than a besom from the birch tree,' he thought, and he dragged a stone to the tree and climbed upon it. Then he reached up to the hole. He was not so silly as to put his fist into the bees' nest. No! He knew something about stings; so he parleyed with the bees.

'You bees there,' he called. 'If you give me a piece of honeycomb, I'll give you something.'

He listened for a reply, but he could only hear a deep hum-rum-hum as the bees flew into the darkness and came out again to the light.

'You bees! Did you hear me? I'm Sam Pig. I said I would give you something in exchange for your honey-comb.'

Still the bees buzzed, and he couldn't understand their talk.

'I think they say, "Well, give it, Sam Pig," so I'll give it.'

He picked a great bunch of wild thyme and clover, and laid it at the foot of the tree.

'There you are,' said he. 'Now give me my honey-comb.'

He dipped his hand very carefully into the hollow and broke off a big piece of honeycomb. The bees were so busy tasting the thyme and clover they took no notice of the gentle movement of Sam Pig's hand which moved soft as a little wind blowing inside the nest.

'Thank you, bees,' said Sam politely.

He climbed down and nibbled the honeycomb. Then, singing to himself, he wandered in the wood.

'An acorn from the oak,
A besom from the birch.
Honey from the bee
For me,'

he chanted.

He walked through a marshy place where the rushes grew in thick green patches and the frogs leapt out of his way.

'Have you ever seen a silver birch tree?' he asked the frogs. They shook their heads and winked their beady eyes at him, and then they dived into the water without speaking.

'No, you haven't,' said Sam.

He gathered a bunch of rushes and peeled them so that they became long white strips of pith, light as air, delicate as a fairy's whip. He broke off a branch from an elder tree and slipped them through a cut in the stem to make a cat-o'-nine-tails. Then he ran with the white streamers fluttering like silver ribbons, as the wind caught them and turned them.

Away he ran, careless of his direction, forgetting the dangers of the wood, singing, shouting, nibbling his honeycomb, glancing about now and then to find a silver birch tree.

On a stump in a dark hollow he saw a fox sitting, spectacles on nose, staring up at a board on a tree.

'Hello, Mister Fox,' said Sam boldly. 'What's that you're reading?'

The fox took no notice, but gazed up at the tree.

'Hello, Mister Fox. What's that you're reading?' asked Sam Pig.

Again the fox said nothing, but the hairs in his tail twitched and his whiskers quivered.

'Hello, Mister Fox. Are you deaf? What's that you're reading?'

The fox didn't look at Sam but he saw everything, even the honeycomb sticking out of Sam's pocket.

'Foolish old Fox,
Give him hard knocks,
Flay him, slay him,
Shut him in a box,'

sang Samuel Pig, and he whipped the air with his cat-o'-nine-tails and danced on one leg.

Then the fox gave a bark like an angry dog, and with a sudden spring he caught Sam Pig and held him by the ear.

'Sing that again, Sam Pig. I want to hear that little song,' said he, pulling Sam's ear until the poor pig squeaked in pain.

So Sam sang again in a thin high voice, but he changed the words, he was in such a fright.

'Dear Mister Fox,
He needs a Christmas box,
A coat and a hat
And a pair of yellow socks,'

murmured Sam.

'It doesn't sound quite the same to me,' said the fox, snapping his teeth, 'but it's a nice little song and mind you bring me those things at Christmas.'

'Now, tell me what you are doing here in my part of the wood. "Trespassers will be prosecuted." That's what I was reading.' He pointed to the board fastened on the tree above their heads. 'That means you can't come here unless you pay for trespassing.'

Sam Pig drew the honeycomb from his pocket and offered it to the fox, who snapped it up in a minute and licked his lips.

'Hm! That's good. I want some more. Where did you find it, Sam Pig?'

'In the honey tree, Mister Fox,' said Sam.

'I know an oak tree and a sycamore tree, a crab tree and a larch tree, but I don't know any honey tree,' said the fox.

'I'll show you the honey tree if you'll show me a silver birch,' said Sam.

'Oh, indeed! You must find that for yourself. Come along and take me to the honey tree,' said the fox, and he pulled Sam's ear till it seemed to stretch as long as his tail.

He stumbled through the wood, to the tree where the bees were buzzing angrily.

'That's the honey tree,' said Sam, backing away from it. 'You dip your fist inside, Mister Fox, and the bees will give you some honey.'

The fox had no need of a stone to reach it. He stood on his hind legs, pushed in his paw and scooped with quick jerky grabs at the comb which lined the hollow.

'Here he is. Here's a robber taking our food and giving nothing in return. The other gave us sweet flowers, but this one takes without asking,' cried the bees in a loud hum-hum-buzz.

They flew down in an angry swarm, settling on the

fox's nose, stinging his paws, creeping into his fur, biting the end of his tail, his ears, his jaws.

The fox ran away as fast as he could, yelping and crying with pain. He plunged in the water in the swamp and lay there till the bees flew away. Then, bedraggled and cold and dirty he slouched home.

'That comes of listening to a silly little pig,' he grumbled. 'Never again. I won't bemean myself by speaking to him.'

As for Sam he ran helter-skelter, here and there, bumping his head into the tree-trunks, falling down rabbit holes, stumbling over the blackberry bushes. At last when he had left the angry bees and the fox far behind he sat down on a tuffet of moss to recover his breath.

'A near squeak,' said he to himself. 'Why can't I be left in peace? There was I lying in the sunshine, happy as could be, and now I'm a hunted fugitive.'

He lay down on his back and folded his hands across his fat little chest. Above him the leaves rustled and murmured, whispering secrets which Sam Pig couldn't understand. He liked the voices of the tree and he stared up at the delicate branches which scarcely concealed the sky.

'A sensible tree,' murmured Sam approvingly as the sunlight streamed through and warmed his cheeks. 'Not too leafy and not too big, and it lets the sun come through; I believe I could climb it.'

He looked at the papery white trunk of the tree and then slowly raised his eyes to the branches with their fine twigs and the slender leaves, shaped like tiny hearts.

'I do believe – I do believe –' he murmured, sitting upright. 'Yes. It isn't an oak tree because there ain't no acorns, and it isn't an elm because there ain't no green pennies. It isn't a crab because there ain't a single apple and it ain't a wild cherry nor a hawthorn nor a holly. It's a silver birch! There's the silver all wrapped round the trunk, bright as a shilling, and there's the birch twigs all ready for besom-making.'

He cut off a bunch of twigs and bound them on a stout sapling to make a little besom. Then he wandered slowly home, brushing the dead leaves from the wood as he went, piling them in little heaps ready for the hedgehog's bed or the badger's mattress.

'Wherever have you been?' asked Ann when he opened the door. 'You've been away since breakfast and now it's tea-time.'

'Ah,' sighed Sam Pig. 'When you send me besom-hunting, you must give me a sword and a suit of armour. I've been nearly killed by an old fox and a lot of bees.'

'You've found a lovely besom brush,' said Bill. 'It will do to sweep up the garden.'

'And to whisk the eggs,' said Tom, the cook.

'And to brush the floors,' said Ann.

'And I found a honey tree,' Sam informed them proudly. 'I know how to get honey without disturbing the bee-folk. I'll get you some pieces of comb tomorrow when they've recovered from Mister Fox's visit.'

'And I will make a pudding with it,' Ann told them all.

Sam went out to get the honeycomb the next day and the bees let him take all he wanted. Ann made the pudding and Sam beat the eggs with the silver birch besom. It tasted of silver birch and wood smoke and honey mixed, which is the nicest flavour a pudding can have. At least that is what Sam Pig thought as he ate it.

The Keys of the Trees

'Riddle-me, Riddle-me, Ree.
In my pocket I carry a key. . . .'

So sang the West Wind as he blustered through the wood, with his hair flying and his fingers jingling something in his pocket.

Little John Bunting stood still, listening to the Wind's voice. He scratched his head thoughtfully, and tried to guess the riddle-me-ree, but he couldn't find the answer.

'I gives it up,' said he, and he turned his back on the Wind and walked towards home.

'Riddle-me, Riddle-me, Ree.
'Twill unlock a sycamore tree,'

chanted the West Wind, blowing John's hair awry, and throwing a bunch of sycamore keys on the ground as he flew by.

John picked them up, looked at the green-winged

fruits, shook them so that they rattled together, and put them in his pocket. 'Keys are keys,' said he to himself, 'and if they won't unlock one thing, they'll maybe unlock another.'

When he got home he tried them on the house door, but there was the big iron key in the lock, so they were not needed. He went to wind up the clock, but the spindly-shanked key lay on the shelf, and his sycamore keys were no use. He tried to unlock his money-box, but the keyhole was too small for these double keys from the trees.

He sat down by the fire and pulled one to pieces with careful fingers. He took off the veined wing and opened the knob.

Inside was a curled-up green leaf, double, like the key itself. Whatever could he do with a key like this? What would it open? It was neither a door key, nor a clock key, nor a money-box key. It wouldn't open the jam-cupboard, the oak chest, or the garden gate.

But the Wind blew through the crack in the door, shouting shrilly:

'Riddle-me, Riddle-me, Ree.
'Twill unlock a sycamore tree!'

Dusk had already fallen, and John Bunting's father came home with his axe from his work in the great woods which spread over the hillside. Mrs Bunting lighted the lamp, and John ran to feed the goats before it was quite dark. He shut them in the shed for the night, but he could not lock even that door with his sycamore keys.

'Tell me, Father,' he said, as he sat down at the tea-table

between his parents. 'Tell me, what is there inside a sycamore tree?'

'There's nothing but timber, John Boy,' replied his father, munching his bread and jam. 'It's good wood, sycamore, and it's a fine tree. You can always know it, even when it's dark, by the feel of the trunk. An oak's rough and warm, like a man, and a beech is smooth and cool, like a lady, but a sycamore is scaly like a great fish and rippled as water.'

He helped himself to more jam, and continued: 'It's a tree like the letter Y, every twig like a Y, every branch forked. It's got a few secrets, has the sycamore tree.'

John felt very curious about the tree which could be unlocked by the strange keys which he had in his pocket.

The next morning he went to the fields to help his father.

'Which is a sycamore tree, Father?' he asked.

'That yon's a sycamore,' said Mr Bunting, pointing to a great tree which stood alone in the hedge.

John ran to the tree and searched for a lock in its scaly green trunk. He hunted high and low, peering into the crusts of the surface, dislodging lichen and moss as he fumbled about. At last he saw a narrow crack with a spider's web drawn across it. He put his sycamore key in the hole and turned it. There was a click! and a portion of the trunk swung back to reveal a small crevice, a cupboard in the tree.

It seemed at first to be quite empty, there was nothing inside but a pale light, like the reflection in a mirror. John put his finger there and rubbed the cool smooth walls. Then he touched the little gleaming spot, which flickered and shone like a sunbeam. It was a jewel he could not hold, for it slipped through his fingers like water.

It was a little picture of summer, hidden away in the sycamore tree's heart, a piece of a summer day, captured by that great tree, and kept there in secret for the winter months. It was a shiny, lovely thing, just a bit of blue sky and sunshine falling through leaves, dappling a field bright with flowers. A pond lay in the grass, and on it swam three white ducks, their feet paddling the cool depths. In the bough overhanging the water a cuckoo sang: 'Cuckoo! Cuckoo!' and the faint sound of its voice came to the boy as he stared at the beauty of the summer's day, hidden in the tree.

He turned round suddenly, to see if the picture was a reflection. No, the sky was grey and sunless, the meadow was rough grass, unglistening, half-asleep in the late autumn, and a cold wind blew across the dark pond, ruffling it to blackness. Yet when he turned to the tree again all was motion and light and glitter in the little cupboard he had unlocked.

The West Wind banged the door with a loud clatter, and John could not open it again.

'I shan't forget,' said he. 'I know why it is such a happy tree. It is because it has summer in its heart.' Then he dug a hole in the bank and planted his keys there.

> *'Riddle-me, Riddle-me, Ree.*
> *In my pocket I carry a key,'*

called the Wind, bustling through the wood, and knocking on all the tree-trunks as if they were doors and he was the postman.

John Bunting listened to the Wind's cry.

'I can't guess that riddle. I gives it up,' he replied, and he stood very still on the pathway, waiting for the Wind's answer. The Wind came rushing up to him, blowing through his thin trousers, and sending a shiver through his bones.

'Riddle-me, Riddle-me, Ree.
'Twill unlock an ashen tree,'

sang the West Wind, and he threw a bunch of ash keys at John's feet.

John picked up the green bunch and examined the strangely twisted keys.

'I will try them on the ash trees,' said he to himself, and he ran home.

He waited till he had chopped the firewood, and roosted the hens and locked the door to keep out the fox. Then, when he sat by the kitchen fire with his father and mother, he spoke out his thoughts:

'Tell me, Father,' said he. 'Tell me, what is there in an ash tree?'

'There's nothing but timber, John Boy,' replied his father, lighting his pipe. 'It's good wood, ash, strong, tough wood, which we use for making rakes and fork-tails. You can always tell it by its greyness and smoothness, and it's grand for burning on the fire! In the dark I know an ash tree by the sound of its leaves moving like water flowing.'

'It's a fairy tree,' added his mother. 'My grandfather used ash leaves to cure people, just by touching them. It's a lovely tree, the ash.' She laughed softly as if she knew more than she would say.

John fondled the keys in his pocket.

The next day he went to the fields to help his father as usual.

'Which is an ash tree, Father?' he asked.

'There's an ash, yonder,' replied Mr Bunting, and he showed his son a graceful tree in the middle of the field. Its branches were bare, and its grey twigs held up their long black-tipped fingers to the sky.

John ran to the tree and hunted for the lock. He moved his hands through the crevices of the lattice-trunk, seeking among the diamond-shaped spaces for a lock which would take the Wind's keys.

He found the keyhole, and inserted his winged ash key. He turned the twisty handle, and the bark sprang back, revealing a little cupboard of grey wood.

It seemed to be quite empty, but as he stood peeping there, a murmur of sweet music came to him. He heard a lovely song, a cascade of melody, now high, now so deep the sound faded, exquisite as the notes of a nightingale. It was the heart of the tree singing for happiness.

The boy put his ear to the tree, and listened enchanted by the music. He saw the shadow of a harp on the tree's trunk, and the strings moved as the song grew stronger, till a great organ sound came beating on the air.

John closed the door, and walked slowly away, with many a glance over his shoulder at the stately tree whose soul was full of music.

'I shan't forget,' said he. 'That's why Mother called it a fairy tree,' and he planted his keys in the hedgerow.

Once again John Bunting was walking in the wood when he heard the West Wind roaring and shaking the trees. He whistled down the branches, and shook the twigs till they rattled like dice in a box.

'Riddle-me, Riddle-me, Ree.
In my pocket I carry a key,'

he shouted with a mighty voice.

John laughed and threw his cap in the air for the Wind to catch.

'I gives it up,' he called at once. 'Wind, I gives it up. Give me the key, Wind.'

'Riddle-me, Riddle-me, Ree.
'Twill unlock an oaken tree,'

sang the Wind, as he buffeted John and tossed his cap into the bushes. He ran, and the Wind flung a handful of brown acorns after him.

'These aren't keys! These are ordinary acorns. They won't unlock anything, I'm sure,' said he, but the Wind bellowed:

'Riddle-me, Riddle-me, Ree.
'Twill unlock an oaken tree!'

'I know an oak tree,' said John. 'Every boy in England knows an oak tree,' and he ran along the wood path, trying the acorns on the sapling oaks which grew among the beeches and spruce. No tree had anything like a key-hole, and so he went home to tea.

He fed the dog, and gathered the eggs and did his nightly work. Then he locked all up, but never a keyhole was large enough for the acorns the Wind had given him.

'Tell me, Father,' said he, when his father had taken off his boots and was resting after his day's labour. 'Tell me, what is there in an oak tree?'

'There's nothing but timber, John Boy,' answered his

father, and he leaned back in his chair and stretched out his feet to the blaze.

'That's a log of oak on the fire now,' he continued. 'It's the best wood there is – strong as steel. They used to make our battleships of it in days gone by, I've heard tell. You can always know oak by its sturdiness, and the roughness of its bark, and by the warmth and hardness. If you put your hand on an oak in the dark of night you can feel a warmth coming from it, as all animals know.'

'There are lots of oaks near the pathway through the wood,' said John.

'They're only young ones, babies you know, about fifty years old. I'll show you an oak tomorrow, an oak that's five hundred years old.'

'Five hundred!' cried John. 'Why it was here when – it was here when – when – why Father, it was here when – It was here in the fifteenth century.'

'And what happened then?' asked Mrs Bunting.

'I'm sure I don't know,' said her husband. 'All I remember of my school days is William the Conqueror, 1066.'

'I've forgotten too,' laughed John.

'I'll bet the tree hasn't forgotten,' Mr Bunting muttered. 'They remember. I know that. They remember.'

The next day father and son went off together, John full of excitement to see the ancient oak. It stood at a crossroad, like a gnarled old warrior guarding the four ways.

As John stood watching it a motor-car rushed by, followed by a bus and a lorry, but the tree stood with its serene gaze staring back through the centuries.

John waited till all was quiet, and then he hunted for the keyhole. He found a rounded hole, almost out of his reach, so he climbed on a stone and pressed close to the tree. He turned the acorn lock, and with a deep groan the tree opened its immense side. There lay the cupboard, the tiny space revealed in the tree's heart, bare and empty, but when John rubbed his fingers over the warm cream-coloured wood, he saw a picture reflected there, coloured brightly, with moving figures as if a magic mirror gave back the movements of people who had once passed along the road.

A lady in a full rose-coloured surcoat and peacock gown walked past. On her head she wore a high-pointed hat with a delicate gauzy veil which fluttered in the wind. With her walked a kind-faced countrywoman, her neck and head swathed in a white wimple and hood, her stout body bulky with the thick dress she wore. Behind this pair came a friar, his eyes to the ground, and John noticed even the footprints of their long shoes, and the mark of the countrywoman's stick as they passed the tree.

Then a swineherd in ragged leather coat drove a herd of long-legged ravenous pigs towards the oak, and they guzzled the acorns which lay scattered on the grass. John turned abruptly as he heard their squeals and cries, but nothing was there, only a robin which sang shrilly as it sat near on a bough and watched the boy with inquisitive eyes.

John turned back to the ever-changing picture inside the tree. There was a clatter of hooves, and a horseman rode by, his armour flashing, and the harness jingling with bright metal. The swineherd fled, and the pigs scurried from the horse's feet. John too sprang from his stone in a hurry. Down the road came a labourer sitting sideways on a cart-horse, which lifted its great feet proudly, conscious of the tinkling bells and the brasses on its face.

The man nodded to John. 'Good day,' said he, and John nodded back: 'How do, Bob.'

He climbed up to the tree again, but the door was shut, the keyhole had gone. The tree gazed along the broad roads, to north, south, east, and west, watching the traffic of town and country, but all the time dreaming in its heart of the days of its youth five hundred years ago.

'Only the oak remembers,' said John, stroking the scarred and weathered old trunk. 'I know why the oak is such a mighty tree. It is because it has lived for so long and remembered the past.'

Then he planted the acorns in a clearing, and went back to the fields to help his father.

Sam Pig and the Hurdy-Gurdy Man

THE little country road linked village to hamlet, and along it travelled farmers' carts, wagons, horses, and ordinary people going about their daily business. Fields stretched on either side, with hedges of wild roses and bitter-sweet, with ditches of meadow-sweet and rushes. The road ran like a white ribbon in the green countryside.

Along this road one summer's day there came a small figure in check trousers and wide sun-hat. By his way of walking anyone could recognize little Sam Pig. Usually Sam took the field paths, the tracks used by animals, the lonely ways where the only folk one would meet were foxes and hedgehogs and tramps and pedlars and farm men. This day Sam went on the road for a special reason. He walked at a good pace, keeping close to the hedge, singing a song, dancing a few steps now and then, calling to bird and beast in the field.

The hedge came to an end, and a low stone wall

began. It was a very old wall, green with stonecrops and ferns, rosy with Robin-run-in-the-hedge, and purple with toad flax. The flowers made a patchwork of colour on the ancient wall. The stones were bound together by a tangled web of roots and flowers which had grown there undisturbed for a hundred years.

Sam Pig sat down on this little wall. It was so low he could rest his feet on the ground. It was as comfortable as an easy chair, with its mossy-cushioned stones.

Sam took a small notebook and a pencil from his pocket.

He was going to write down all the things that passed along the road that morning. He sat there waiting, watching the bend in the road. It was very quiet, with only the sound of the river murmuring as it fell over the distant rocks, and the hum of the insects in the grasses.

Sam licked the pencil and waited. After a long time a cart came slowly along the road, and Sam wrote down 'cart'. Next came a high-wheeled yellow gig with a prancing horse, well groomed and beautiful. Sam noted it in his book, in his own special writing. After another long wait came an ancient motor-car, and then a donkey-cart. So the country traffic moved along that winding road among wild roses and violets, and some people nodded to Sam, and cried 'How'do?' and others never saw him at all. He sat very still, like a part of the lichened mossy wall, intent on his work, and naturally it took a long time to write each word.

Of course Sam didn't write as you and I write, for he had never been to school. He made little pictures, which were just as good as words and twice as nice. There was a square cart for the farmer's cart, and a long cart for the brewer's dray, and a couple of little wheels for a bicycle. The best word was the donkey-cart, but Sam made a rag-bag for a beggar who lurched past and a sunbonnet for a little girl who dawdled along with many a backward glance at little Sam sitting on the wall.

Well, Sam made the list, and he was thinking of going home to show it to Brock when somebody else came along the road. It was a humped figure who limped very slowly.

'I'll wait for this one and then I'll go,' said Sam, licking his pencil hopefully. He had seen neither wizard nor fairy nor giant. They don't walk the highroads in these days, and Sam was curious about this creature coming. Then Sam saw that the hump was a kind of box the stranger carried, slung on his shoulder by a strap. There was a wooden leg attached to it. Sam was so much excited over this box, with its painted front, that he forgot to write anything in his book.

The man came up to him and stopped. He slipped the strap from his shoulder and took off his old green hat. He looked very tired and dusty.

'A hot day, mate,' he remarked. 'Hot work carrying all this 'ere.'

'Yes, sir,' said Sam.

'Can you guess what this is?' continued the man.

'No, sir,' said Sam.

'It's a hurdy-gurdy. Have you ever seen a hurdy-gurdy, my lad?'

'No, sir,' said Sam, his eyes popping with wonder.

The man sat down on the wall by Sam's side. He wiped his face and neck with his red handkerchief, and Sam saw how thin and weary he was.

'I could do with a drink. I'm parched. How far is it to the next village, mate?' asked the man.

'A few miles,' said Sam. 'I could get you a drink if you've got a cup, sir.'

The man opened a sack and took out an enamel mug. Sam ran off to the field close by where there was a spring of fresh cold water, icy from the depths of the earth. He carried it carefully to the thirsty hurdy-gurdy man.

'Thank you. Thank you, mate. I've not tasted water like this spring water since I was a little nipper like you living in the country,' said the man. Then he hesitated and peered at Sam more closely.

'Well, not like you, for I must say you've got big ears and an uncommonly ugly face.'

'Yes, sir,' said Sam.

The man drained the mug and put it away.

'Now, for that little attention, I'll tell you what I'll do. I'll play you a tune on my hurdy-gurdy. Would you like that?'

'Oh yes, sir,' said Sam, clapping his hands.

So the man put the wooden leg under the hurdy-gurdy and turned the handle. Such a jolly tune came rippling out, in a fountain of little notes, Sam could hardly keep himself from dancing. But the lovely music went wrong, it stammered, and some notes dropped away, and others ran into one another. The hurdy-gurdy was old, its tunes were cracked, its best days were done. It tried hard, but it couldn't manage. It was a pity, for it was a very nice old hurdy-gurdy.

'Well, I must be going, mate,' said the man, rising slowly to his feet. 'I'm tired and I could sit here all today and all tomorrow. I could sleep here.'

'Why don't you?' asked Sam.

'I've got my living to earn, my bread and cheese and drop of beer.'

He hoisted the box on his shoulder, and took up the sack. He looked so tired Sam was sorry for him.

'Would you like someone to help you?' asked Sam timidly.

'Well, I should, but I can't pay anything. I've taken nothing today, and that water is the first drink that has passed my lips. I must get on to the village and earn my meat.'

'I'll go with you,' said Sam. 'I can help a bit.'

So away with the hurdy-gurdy man went Sam. The little pig wasn't afraid, for the man's face was kind.

Sam carried the sack, which held the mug, a clean shirt, and a pair of Sunday trousers. They talked as they went along – at least the man talked and Sam listened. He told Sam about the places he had seen on the road, little stone Cotswold villages, and beautiful towns, and slow-moving rivers, and deep woods. He had played his hurdy-gurdy in every village and now he was moving north to the hills and high moors and wild rivers.

As he talked they came to the gates of the Big House, and they both stared up the drive.

'Will you play there?' asked Sam hopefully. 'If we can get past the lodge safely, we can play to the cook. She's a friend of mine, an Irishwoman.'

The lodge-keeper wasn't in sight, so they went through the massive gates and up the long drive to the Big House. Sam led the way to the back door. The hurdy-gurdy man set up his musical box and turned the handle. The gay, crooked, broken little tunes came tumbling out. They were lovely and they were wrong, tantalizing with their confusion. The cook came to the door, and after her came the two little blue-clad kitchen-maids.

'Glory be, I bethought me 'twas the little pigs squealing here, and they afther being killt,' said she. 'I'll give ye a penny to go away with that hurdy-gurdy of yours, me man.'

Then she caught sight of little Sam Pig, smiling up at her with his wide mouth and innocent blue eyes.

'Arrah! If it isn't the little Pigwiggin! If it isn't the little cretur as fell into the puddin' bowl and got mistook for a Leprechaun an' all! Indade, and it's welcome you are, and plase to forget the hard words I said about your organ there. Your tunes are in need of a plumber, I'm thinking. It's tarrible quare they are, lepping about like a mad Mooley cow.'

'I thought you would like to hear the music,' said Sam disappointedly.

'Indade an' I do. But if the misthress hears ever a squeak of it she'll be afther sending you off double quick. So hould your whist a minute while I'm afther getting you a sup of tay and a bite. Come ye in.'

They followed the kind cook down the stone passage to the big kitchen. They sat down by the fire and she made them tea and gave them food. The hurdy-gurdy man ate ravenously, and the cook looked pityingly at him.

'It's famished ye are. You look tired to the bone,' said she.

'Nay, I've got my living to earn. I can't lay up,' said the man.

She got her purse from the kitchen drawer and gave him a few pence. Then she sent him on his way.

'Good-bye, hurdy-gurdy man. Good-bye, little Pig-wiggin, and God be with you,' said she.

They went down the drive, but the lodge-keeper was waiting for them with angry words. They went to the village, but everybody was too busy to give money to a cracked old hurdy-gurdy. Sam held out the mug and rattled a penny in it, but at the end of the day there was only fivepence in it.

'You'd best be going home, young Sam,' said the hurdy-gurdy man. 'Thank you for your company. You've helped me quite a lot.'

'What will you do, Mister Hurdy-gurdy man?'

'Oh, I shall have a bite and then sleep under the hedge and struggle on,' said the man wearily.

'I know a nice place for you. I know a barn with hay in it. Would you like that?' asked Sam.

'I should indeed,' said the man.

'Then I'll wait while you have your supper and I'll take you there. It's at Woodseats Farm, where Farmer Greensleeves lives. He's a friend of mine, like Sally and all of them.'

'Well, that would suit me down to the ground,' said the man.

He went to the inn and had his bread and cheese. Then he walked back with Sam. This time they went by the little paths, on grass that was soft to the man's feet.

Sam saw the farmer, and he ran across to ask permission.

'Of course, Sam Pig, any friend of yours is welcome,' said Farmer Greensleeves affably. So Sam took the hurdy-gurdy man to the big barn, and fetched him a mug of milk and a hunch of cake from the farmhouse.

'I shall be all right tomorrow, Sam,' said the man, lying down in the sweet-smelling hay. 'A good night will set me up.'

'There's just one thing,' said Sam. 'Will you lend me the hurdy-gurdy for tonight? I want to play to my brothers. I'll bring it back tomorrow.'

'Yes, take it. It's so cracked you can't make it any worse. Take it, Sam,' said the man, and he fell asleep.

Sam staggered slowly away with the hurdy-gurdy on his back. It took a long time to get home, but he was excited at the thought of the surprise he had in store for Brock and the family.

He walked softly up the path, set up the hurdy-gurdy, and began to play. The door was flung open, and the three little pigs came tumbling out, shrieking with joy.

'Good gracious, Sam! You did startle us! What is this magical box? Oh how lively it is! Let me try,' they called, and they took turns to wind the handle and the little cracked tunes came jumbling out higgledy-piggledy to their delight.

'Sam,' said Brock as he listened. 'It sounds a bit cracked to me.'

'Never mind. We love it,' said the pigs.

'I think that hurdy-gurdy has seen its best days. It must be fifty years old,' said Brock, looking at it.

'We love it,' said the pigs again.

All evening they played, but when the sun went down and they came in to supper, Brock took the hurdy-gurdy to pieces. He worked at it for an hour and then he carried it off to the woods.

'I'll put some new tunes in this hurdy-gurdy,' he thought.

He let the wind blow into it, and the nightingale sing into it. He let the brook murmur by it, and the trees rustle there. Then he brought it back to the house.

'Play one more tune before we go to bed,' begged the little pigs.

'All right. Now listen,' said Brock. He turned the handle and the most lovely music came out, far sweeter and clearer than ever before. Nothing cracked or false was left. The Badger had put the music of the woods into the old hurdy-gurdy. There was a nightingale singing in the background, and a blackbird fluting to a song. There was sunshine and May Day in it. There was the harp of the trees, and the murmur of wind and water all mingled with the original airs of the little organ.

'What have you done?' asked Sam. 'It's quite different. It's beautiful now.'

'I've mended it,' said Brock. 'If I can mend broken whistles and broken hearts, I can surely mend a broken hurdy-gurdy.'

Sam carried it back to the barn the next morning. The hurdy-gurdy man was asleep, but he awoke when Sam opened the door and let in a flood of sunshine.

'How have you slept?' asked Sam.

'Champion! I feel a different man. I can face anything now,' said the man, stretching himself and standing up to shake the hay from his hair.

'Let's go to the farm and play them a tune,' said Sam. 'It will please them.'

'Maybe they won't be so pleased when they hear my poor old hurdy-gurdy,' laughed the man ruefully.

They walked across to the farmhouse and the man played the hurdy-gurdy.

'What have ye done to it?' he asked, as he turned the handle. 'Nay, this is a fair treat to listen to. It's all changed. It's better than ever it was. There are the old tunes made lovely. What have ye done?' he asked amazed.

'It was Brock the Badger who did it,' said Sam. 'He mended it for you. He said you would never lack money or friends while you played those tunes, for they will bring back good days to the memory of listeners. He said all the world will want to hear your hurdy-gurdy now.'

It was true. The hurdy-gurdy man never lacked a kind friend and money in his purse. He went through all the villages in England and Ireland, playing his tunes to the people, and giving joy to the listeners. Every year he came back to the farm, and then Sam Pig and Brock the Badger met him and heard his tales, and turned the handle of the little hurdy-gurdy for their own pleasure. Out came the rippling dancing tunes which made the children dance and the women smile in every cottage of the land.

Upon Paul's Steeple

LONG long ago, when girls sold lavender in London streets, crying 'Who'll buy my lavender?' as they held up bunches of the scented flowers, and men sang 'Old chairs to mend' as they passed along the roads with bundles of rushes under their arms, long ago when there were no buses and cars, but great horses pranced down the streets, and little boys and girls came running out of their homes to play whips and tops and ninepins and marbles, in Whitehall, where the King's palace stood, long ago, a strange thing happened.

A dove flew over London streets and gardens. It rested on the top of Saint Paul's steeple, and this, you must know, was old Saint Paul's, for it was before the time of the great fire which destroyed so many of the London churches. In its beak the dove carried a seed, which it had brought from an orchard in Kent. The dove sat there, contemplating the shining river, the Tower of London, the palaces, the forest of steeples, and it thought all those slender spires were trees of stone growing among the wooden houses of old London.

It cooed contentedly as it gazed at the fair view, and the seed dropped from its beak. Then the dove rose on grey wings and flew away to other woods.

The seed fell in a pocket of soil, and there, sheltered by a tiny rail on the top of the steeple, warmed by the sun, refreshed by the dew, it grew. In time the little brown scale burst. A crooked white root pressed down, and a white stem pressed up, and after many months little green leaves appeared. The rootlets crept lower and lower, grasping like hands at the stones on the steeple, clinging to crevices, poking their tendrils into every nook and cranny. The plant grew taller and stronger and bolder as the years went by. It was so high up nobody noticed it, but the other steeples had seen it, and they talked with their bells about the green shoot on the top of Saint Paul's.

'Orange and lemon,' called the bells of Saint Clement. 'Is it an orange tree or a lemon tree I see growing there?' All the bells jingled and jangled in the mornings and evenings, telling one another about the wonderful tree growing high above the city.

At last an astronomer, gazing at the Evening Star with his telescope, saw something strange at the top of Saint Paul's. He twiddled the eyepiece and stared again.

'What's that? A tree? A tree on the top of Saint Paul's steeple?'

He looked again, and exclaimed, 'An apple tree! I can see little green apples growing up there! A marvel! A wonder!'

Then all London came to look at the sight, and people

bought little spyglasses to peep, and a man did a roaring trade by hiring a telescope and letting citizens look through it at a penny a spy. There was no doubt it was an apple tree, but whether it was a good or evil omen, nobody knew.

The tree grew fast in the clear air, and spread out its green branches to the sunlight.

'Cut it down,' cried some of the burgesses of London. 'It will harm the church.' 'Leave it alone,' said the Dean. 'It's a miracle. It is to remind us of Adam and Eve and the apple.' So the tree was left to grow, and it spread its lovely web of branches over the roof of the great church, like a green tent.

The next spring it was a garden of pink and white flowers against the blue of the sky, a silken tissue of blooms, and the petals fell on the roof and on the streets, and made a carpet of colour. The robin and the chaffinch built their nests up there, and the music of the birds rang above the noise of men and horses in the cobbled streets below.

In summer the tree was covered with thousands of little green apples. Some of them were blown off and bounced on the heads of the passers-by, but the choirboys picked up most of the windfalls and carried them to feed the swine in the royal piggeries down by the river.

In autumn the fruit ripened, and the branches of the great tree drooped over London with a weight of red and golden apples.

The little boys came running as soon as school was over, from all the streets of London, up the hill of Ludgate, down the street of Fleet, carrying baskets and sticks, bags and crooks, to try to hook the lowest branches. The watchman prevented them from throwing stones lest the precious windows of Saint Paul's should be broken.

From many a little wooden house in London came the smell of apples roast, apples baked, apples in pies, and apples in dumplings, and every spice shop was sold out of cloves. They were the sweetest, nicest apples anyone had ever tasted, and even King Charles had apple-pasties.

When the bells rang for matins, the great waves of sound, the 'Ting-tong-tangle' of great Saint Paul's which rose in such magnificent peals in the air, shook the boughs, and rosy apples came bumping down. When the bells were silent, the tree stopped quivering, and the apples hung like the glittering balls on a Christmas tree, far above anyone's reach.

Now among the children who hurried to Saint Paul's tree was a little waif named Giles. He had no parents, or anyone to care for him, in all the great city. Giles was a chimney-sweep, and he had to climb chimneys in the dark of the cold mornings, whilst his master stood down below in comfort, and urged him forward in the soot and the terrible blackness of the tight, twisty, narrow chimneys of old London.

He was always cold, always hungry, always dirty, except when he could slide into the river and bathe, which was never more than once a year. He ran off to pick the apples from under Saint Paul's but when he arrived there were none left. He went sadly home to the hovel where he lived, for he must try to sleep before dawn, when his work began.

He lay thinking of the apple tree during the night, and at last he stole from his mattress and crept over his sleeping master. He sidled through the door, and away to find apples by moonlight. He ran barefoot through the streets till he reached the churchyard. There was the mighty tree, a canopy of leaves, and through its branches the moon shone like another golden apple.

Giles began to climb. He scrambled up the sides of the church along the buttresses, for he was agile as a monkey through years of climbing the tortuous chimneys. Saint Paul himself put out a hand of stone and gave him a lift. Saint Gabriel tilted a carved and chiselled wing and raised him further. Saint Thomas lifted him in his arms above the danger points, and Saint John carried him to the roof.

Giles scrambled up the leaden roof and reached the spire. A branch dipped with the wind, and he clung to it. From bough to trunk he climbed, and then up the ladder of the branches till his head came out at the top, and he looked down at the leaves below him. He picked the dusky apples hiding in the dark leaves, and then, when his hunger was satisfied, he stared at London, at the houses and towers and London Bridge, at the great broad River Thames, at Saint Clement's, and Saint Martin's in its green fields, and Saint Giles, and far away the little villages hidden in groups of trees. His eye wandered to the great ships at anchor, to the barges and boats, the orchards and gardens near the King's palace, the lines of hedgerows near London Bridge.

He had had many a fine view when he poked his head through the tall chimneys of noblemen's houses – but nothing like this. Everywhere was silver in the moonlight, and the river was the most silver of all. Above him was the arch of the sky, and as he sat in his leafy hiding-place he felt he had never seen so many stars. He started to count them, beginning at the Great Bear, which he knew very well, but soon he was dazzled by shooting stars and twinkling stars and bright planets. They seemed to be circling round the apple tree, so he shut his eyes and fell asleep.

At daybreak he awoke, for the birds around him sang and chirruped so loudly sleep was impossible. He watched the golden sun rise in a sky as pink as the legs of the King's flamingoes, and he remembered that he ought to have been inside Lord Howard's chimney at that moment. He chuckled, for he knew his master could never find him up in Saint Paul's apple tree.

He ate apples for breakfast, and apples for dinner, and apples for tea, large rosy apples full of good white flesh and sweet juice. All day he stayed aloft, like a sailor in the Crow's nest, staring down at London, at the soldiers and the beggars, the priests and fine ladies, walking up and down like ants on the earth. Only when the great bells rang he put his arms round the tree for safety, lest he should be tossed like an apple down below.

He was happy for the first time in his life, for he was neither tired, nor hungry, nor afraid of his master. The chiming bells brought songs to him, and as they rang he sang, up and down, keeping time and tune with the bells, his voice drowned by their clamour. Yet when the bells ceased he went on singing. He was so high in the air, like a bird in the tree, he forgot his voice might be heard by those far below.

The next day King Charles rode out of the palace, and went to Saint Paul's. He was proud of the famous apple tree which had so miraculously grown on the steeple, and wanted to see it again in all its glory of fruit and leaf, of green branches and singing birds.

The bells ceased ringing and he sat on his white horse looking up at the tree. Suddenly a sweet high voice came out of the sky, a clear silvery voice fresh as a thrush's, and the words of the song came floating down to the King below, like the chime of a tiny bell.

> '*Upon Paul's steeple stands a tree,*
> *As full of apples as can be.*
> *The little boys of London Town,*
> *They run with hooks to pull them down.*
> *And then they run from hedge to hedge,*
> *Until they come to London Bridge.*'

The tune was that of the bells calling people to church, and the voice was sweet as an angel's.

'What's that?' asked the King. 'One of the Cherubim?'

'It must indeed be a Cherub,' replied the Dean. 'No one could climb up there, your Majesty, unless he had wings.'

Again the song rang through the air, a tinkling bell song, and then the watchers saw something coming slowly down the tree, gliding down the roof of Saint Paul's to the buttresses. Helped by the stone hands and wings of the saints, the boy slipped to the earth, but before he could make off he found himself surrounded by a little crowd of plumed horsemen.

'Faith! 'Tis a black angel,' laughed Charles, and someone grabbed Giles by the collar.

'Who are you, boy, and how did you get up there?' asked the Dean.

'Please, sir, I am Giles the chimney-sweeper, and I climbed up,' said Giles, thoroughly frightened.

The King said a few words privately to the Dean, and then turned to the boy. 'So you are a sweep, and you've climbed a greenleaf chimney! Do you want to go back to your master, my boy?'

'No, sir,' Giles shivered.

'Then you must take your punishment. You have climbed Saint Paul's tree, so now you belong to Saint Paul. You must go to the school of Saint Paul, and sing in the choir of Saint Paul, and will you like that?'

Giles grinned happily. 'Thank you, your Majesty,' said he.

'Now come with me and be bathed and clothed,' said the Dean. 'We must find you some better rags than those you have on, and although we know the sound of your singing, we don't know the colour of your face!'

So Giles was scrubbed and cleaned, and dressed afresh, so that a merry little boy came out from the grime of years. He became a chorister at Saint Paul's, and learned his Latin at Saint Paul's school. His voice was the sweetest, highest voice among all the sweet high voices in the choir, and he was chosen to sing in chant and carol and madrigal.

The King's favourite song was the bell-song which Giles sang up in the apple tree, and many a time the little chorister went to the palace to sing it to His Majesty and his guests.

He stood in his long gown before the courtiers and ladies, and a minstrel rang a chime, in tune with the boy's rhyme:

'Upon Paul's steeple stands a tree,
As full of apples as can be.
The little boys of London Town,
They run with hooks to pull them down.
And then they run from hedge to hedge,
Until they come to London Bridge.'

Then everyone laughed and patted him on the back, and the King gave him a gold penny and sent him back to school.

Sledging

BEFORE we got up we knew the snow had come. We could smell that heavenly manna. We knew from the strange silence in the yard, the muffled thuds of the horse's hooves, the soft roll of cart-wheels, which usually groaned as they were drawn over the sharp stones; we knew from the clear timbre of the voices which seemed to come from disembodied spirits, stepping silently on earth. There was a delicate creamy light on the ceiling and the colour of the walls had subtly changed. The flash of a lantern cut the wall like a scimitar, as somebody carried the light to the milk measuring. We drew back the half-closed heavy curtains and scratched a finger-width in the snow-blossoms which powdered the glass. The snow was heaped on the sill, close to our fingers, snow striving to enter, snow the magician come from the sky, to change our land. The fields were darkling blue, icy and mysterious like an unknown lake in the light of dawn, and we turned our eyes away to more homely, friendly objects in the yard below. In the lantern light the footprints of the men were dark shadowed. Two parallel bars in the snow showed the track of the cart to the loading place. We could see the horse with steaming nostrils standing there, a rug over his back, one foot uplifted, as he pawed the ground. The doors of barn and cart-shed and stable were speckled with drifted snow. The dog peered from the kennel, under the white-covered stone roof.

We dressed hurriedly, pulling on our clothes with tugs of impatience, chattering and shivering and boastful as we broke the ice in the water jug, excitement rising as we plunged our faces into the cold water and heard the ice tinkle in the basin.

We ate our breakfast under the swinging lamp with our eyes gazing out to the clean white undulations of the hillside. The fields were still asleep under the veils of snow, but the house was wide awake and enchanted, for snow had entered to be a guest. The milk was frozen in the dairy, and we held the pieces and tasted them. 'Ice-cream,' we told each other proudly. The floor was wet with the men's feet, and here and there lay a lump of snow fallen from a hob-nailed boot, retaining the impression of the nails. We stooped down between mouthfuls of porridge and cream to pick up a snowy replica of Dan's boot. We tossed a piece of snow in the fire and laughed to hear the hiss of anger as the flames snapped it up. The door was wide open as usual and the wind came through the house like a carving knife, slicing our thin shoulders, cutting our necks, and we wrinkled our faces as we sniffed the piercing ice of the air.

We begged my father to get the sledge ready, but he

took his time. Nothing would hurry him; he had no fear as we had that the snow would go in a minute. Our impatience seemed to act as a brake upon his deliberate movements. He took no notice of us.

We laced up our thick boots and went to the barn for Jesiah to rub dubbin from the grease-pot round their soles. We lifted our feet to the stone bench, and the old man smeared the grease, talking all the time of snowfalls he had known in past days. It wouldn't thaw yet awhile, he assured us. He showed us the robin that always came to the barn and sat among the tools in the corner. It hopped out and fed from his hand, when he held grain for it.

My mother wrapped long scarves or shawls round our necks and tied them in a bundle at the back, so that they were like Victorian bustles. We felt we were putting on armour before going into battle. Already we held snow clasped in our hands, to feel the burning sensation of the fiery snow. We tingled from head to foot as we pressed the white crystals to a hard ball of ice.

We rushed out to the utter silence, shouting to break the intense stillness of the air, the whispering murmur of snow under sunlight, the faint shadows of cat-ice which spread magically over the new-born ice-pools. Ferny edges, leaves of crystal, seemed to grow before us, the long tongues spread out, invisibly moving across to chain the drops of water.

Away we went, leaping the low white wall to the lawn, and tracing our names on the crystalline surface. We plunged into the snow, kicking it in feathery showers, gathering it and eating it and then stooping to make snowballs. Back we went to the flat-topped wall, where we worked at inscribing our identities on the fresh slate before us. We forgot to laugh, we worked solemnly, drawing circles, and squares, and figures of fun, moving along the wall towards the trough.

All morning we toiled at building a snowman, moulding and pressing with feverish haste, tramping paths in the white lawn, churning up the pure whiteness with our heavy little iron-tipped boots. Gradually a man's shape emerged from our piled snow, and we put the head on top. He was awry, sloping backward, and the head was too small for his body, but we snapped little fir-twigs for teeth and placed the besom in his folded arms. We stepped away to view him and found he was perfect.

In the meantime the work of the farm went on, the milk-cart returned with its empty churns, the pigs were cleaned, the horses watered and fed, the mangolds were cut in the chopper and mixed with hay for the cattle. Roots were spread for the sheep, and straw was laid down.

My father appeared from the stable and walked across the yard, stamping his feet to rid them of snow. One hand was in his pocket, he held something there, and we waited to see whether he was going to the barn or the cart-shed, or to the Irishmen's Place. Could he possibly be going to the room we called the 'Master's Chamber'? Was it a key he held down in that pocket's depths?

He stood for a moment to look at our snowman, and we made our appeal.

'The sledge! Father! Are you going to get the sledge?'

He didn't answer. Instead he turned away and slowly mounted the stone stairway leading to his chamber. We glanced meaningly at each other and ran across the lawn, over the wall to the foot of that outside stairway.

'You wait there! There's no need for you to come up.'

We opened our mouths in protest, crying, 'But we – but are you –?'

'Do as I tell you! Wait there! Then you won't get into mischief.'

He walked upward, and stood for a minute or two on the white platform, gazing with his far-seeing blue eyes across the valley to the hills beyond. He stared round the horizon, like a sailor who is at the look-out, and he considered the weather, and watched the sky movements and the set of the wind. He stood with his hands in his pockets, wearing no overcoat, no muffler, no protection from the icy elements.

We curbed our impatience, our longing to climb that stairway, to enter that forbidden chamber, where just because it was forbidden and locked we imagined the most wonderful treasures rested.

He drew the heavy key from his pocket and fitted it in the lock. The door swung open on its well-oiled hinges, but before we could see even the end of the carpenter's bench which stood against the wall, the lower half of the door was shut and the wooden bolt slipped across.

My father disappeared in the dimness, and we stared unspeaking at the snowy steps with his large footprints. The chamber in the high gable had no window, so it was warm with its massive stone walls. The double door opened from the little square platform from which in spring we flew our home-made kites.

From the sounds that came from the room we knew that some repairs were in progress. A nail was hammered in, tools rattled with an enchanting clatter, and a plane spoke with its screeching voice.

We talked in low voices of the coming joy, and we moved away to slide down the milk-cart runway. We wrote our names on the snowy bench, and swept it clean and sat there within sound of the plane, the saw and the hammer.

The door of the chamber opened and we sprang to attention. Our father walked out to the platform with the sledge in his hands. We saw the clean shape of it, the fine curve of the runners, the broad seat, and we let out a great whoop of glee. But he locked the door carefully, and put the key in his jacket pocket, down in those depths among rope ends and grains of corn, and the paper bag of humbugs. He stood for another minute gazing across the valley at the superb scene, where the hills reached up to the dazzling sky, and the black-tipped trees made a frieze in the distant woods. He seemed loath to leave it. Then he lifted his head to the weathercock man, which stood on the gable with outstretched arm, immobile, in blue coat and tight trousers and high top-hat. The two men, farmer and ancient weathercock man, stared at the sky, reading the signs; they listened to the wind and the crackling ice, and they tasted the keen wine of the air. 'How now? Whence comes the wind today?' they seemed to ask that vast sky.

We were dancing with impatience, fearful lest the snow should disappear. Down walked my father, a hand touching the rough wall, steadying his large frame on the steep slippery stones. He went across the yard to the barn and we skipped after, calling to the dog, watching for the robin. He picked up a rope, tested it, and tied it to the sledge. He greased the runners with goosefat and brushed the dust from the seat.

'Here's your sledge, childer, and now be content,' he said.

We dragged the sledge to the kitchen door to show our mother, to remind her to look through the window to see our journeyings, which were to be the swiftest ever known. She told us to be careful and not fall off, and we promised although we knew we should fall many times for care didn't dwell in us. She re-tied the shawl and scarf so tightly that our cheeks bulged and we gasped for breath.

'You're throttling us!' we protested.

We shouted and whooped to cow and horse and servant man as we pulled the sledge round the house to the big gate of the White Field, which was one long slope from the larch wood at the top past the oak wood on its flank to the sunk wall which cut it from the last slope to the river. The upper part was too rough and precipitous for sledging, but there was one long smooth slope which generations of children had used before we were born. It lay below the oak tree, and there we dragged the sledge along the milking track. The oak tree with its wooden bench and swing was our landmark, our starting place for every game, for cricket, for racing, for riding.

We mounted the sledge, shouted to the echo, and stuck in the snow, fast as a fly in treacle. We got off, and tried again, climbing out of snowdrifts, falling into forgotten hollows. At last we found a good track, we rubbed the snow to ice, we pushed with our heels, and as the sledge gathered momentum we swung smoothly down the slope.

One guided, the other clung with arms round the leader's waist, and as we sped we raised our voices to a paean of joy. At the bottom of the field we came to a stop, caught in a snowdrift under the crab-apple tree, or plunged into the holly-bush which waited with prickly arms to receive us. We were breathless with the beat of the wind in our faces. We stared at the parallel marks in the untouched whiteness, proud that we had made them. Then we climbed the hill, dragging the heavy sledge, looking up to see our mother at the window or the servant girl at the trough.

All day we sledged with the brief interval of staggering, snow-caked, home for dinner, when we recounted our falls, our triumphs, our express speed. We stayed out till dusk came down from the woods, and the lamplight shone from the house. The western sky glowed golden, the clouds were painted crimson, and the heavenly windows between the thin clouds were of such a radiance we felt God must be there watching through a gap with His angels by His side. Our hearts were filled with bliss. We wanted the day to go on for ever. The sun set in a crack in the hills, and when we flew on scarlet wings we seemed to go towards that golden ball. We walked backward up the hill, lest we should miss a moment of the lovely frosty pageant which stretched like a banner in the west, and we thought we were the only people on earth who saw it. Never a house but our own was in sight, only fields and woods rising from the river to that splendid sky which was our own possession.

When the sun had gone, and shadows swept over that white bowl of England which was our world, other earthly stars beside our home light shone forth. Here came a beam from a farm in the trees and there a flash from a homestead perched in the hilly woods.

We wrapped the stiffening rope round our hands, and drew the sledge up the tracks. There was ice in the air, and sharp daggers of cold came stabbing from the edge of night. Frozen darkness lay in the dense woods, only we on our exposed slope were irradiated with the after-glow. Then down we went for the last time, and when we sledged in the twilight we felt a wild exhilaration in our veins, we were caught in a web of ice magic. Green swept the west, the crimson clouds turned indigo and darkened to black. Behind us the woods mounted to a blueness which had dropped from the sky over the snow, shadowing it. A planet blazed out and we hailed it with cries of welcome, waving and calling to it. It stared with winking eye and added its light to those of the farmhouse in the trees. More stars appeared in the dome above us, and we felt lonely as we went slowly up the hill. The earth was misted in soft veils, one after another they stole out from hollows and riverside. There was a ghost-stillness, broken only by our voices and the distant bark of a dog. Perhaps it was a wolf, the leader of a pack. Strange beings were abroad, those white shadowless creatures who come with the snow, ice-spirits, demons from the outer air, white-winged birds and snowy beasts who lure travellers to their death.

But we were safe, for our own lighthouse on the hill sent its bright spark to guide us home. A candle was burning in the dairy window, tiny as a glow-worm's beam, and the warm lamplight came from the kitchen, darkening and changing as people passed between it and the uncurtained window. Across the field was the glitter of a lantern at the cow-sheds. We turned our backs on the western sky and faced the lights of home.

I felt such bliss steal over me as I pulled the sledge up the hill that I knew I had reached the core. There could never be anything more beautiful as long as I lived. If only the snow would stay, if the night wouldn't fall, if the lamplight would always shine from the farmhouse to tell me that home was waiting! I could go on for ever, immortal. My happiness was bound up in the presence of that light beaming from the unshuttered window. The vast spaces of the sky, the mystery of snow, the strange sadness of nightfall, were all softened and transformed by that glow from the house. If anyone had closed the shutters we should have been desolate.

Even as I contemplated it, there was the sharp sound of a lifted latch and a golden bar fell on the wall at the door. A shadow stood in the glowing doorway, and a white apron waved and a voice called us.

'Come along in! Tea! Tea! Come along!'

The bronze bell rang, shaken up and down by the wall, and the notes came deep and richly toned to us in the crackling icy air. We hastened, bumping the sledge carelessly along, hurrying home. We opened the gate and shut it with a loud clang which echoed in the hills, so that we banged it again. It told the world that we had finished for the night, we were going home. The stars blinked at the sound of the gate singing across the ether, the blue sky widened, and God turned His eyes to other lands.

We tramped like a couple of explorers across the yard, and dragged the sledge into the brew-house. We stamped our feet like men to rid them of the balling snow. We flung open the kitchen door with a proud gesture. A red glow filled the room, a great fire crackled and sparkled in the frost, the tea-table shone with reflected light, every cup and dish gleaming like a small fire, and the copper and brass on the walls gave out little points of flame.

The smell of hot tea and baked apples assailed our nostrils. We threw off our wet clothes, and the servant girl carried them into the brew-house to dry. We washed our red hands at the sink, exclaiming as the water stung them, and we dried at the common towel behind the door. Then we sat down sighing with comfort at the table, to eat and drink, and boast of our exploits in the land of snow and ice. Tomorrow we would do the same, and the next day and the next. For ever and for ever.

Sam Pig at the Circus

SAM PIG brought back the news. He had seen the picture on an old barn door down the lane. It was one of those ancient doors that act as newspapers or town criers for country-folk. Upon its rough lichened weather-worn surface the auctioneer pasted his bills of sale, which stayed there for a year or more until the wind and rain tore them off. Those who passed by read the words, but as only three or four people went that way on the busiest day, the old door depended upon one telling another the news displayed there.

Now Sam couldn't read the printing, but he was glad the old paper bill had gone and this fresh new one hung on the door. It had brightly coloured letters, green, red, and blue, and a picture. That was clear enough for anybody who couldn't read. Ladies leaping through paper hoops held up by clowns, piebald ponies dancing with their manes flowing, dogs with frills round their necks. Sam climbed the three mossy steps of the barn and stood with his nose close to the poster for a long, long time, smelling the odour of paste, tasting the print, staring at the words. Every detail he saw, every curl and flourish, and the rows of gay letters.

He spelled out the letters which he knew quite well. He didn't know what the word was, but he remembered the alphabet Brock had taught him down by the stream with sticks and pebbles for pen and ink. He said the letters aloud, slowly, choosing the most important-looking word which ran across the poster.

'C for Cabbage. I for Icicle. R for Rain. C for another Cabbage. U for Unicorn. S for Sam and Sally.'

He was pondering this puzzle, of Sam and Sally going to take cabbages to the Unicorn, when he heard a merry sound of laughter. Some children were coming down the lane. Sam retired to the field, through the hedge. He could hear their joyous cries as they read the poster.

'A Circus! A Circus coming to Hemlock Meadow. Ten horses, an eques-es-trian act, a performing seal, a troupe of dogs, and Fairy Bell, the smallest rider in the world with Fairy.'

'I 'specks my Mum and Dad will take me!'

'Hurray! Hurray! I *know* my Dad will take me.'

Sam didn't stop for more.

'I *know* my Brock the Badger will take me,' said he to himself as he galloped over the fields. He ran full-tilt into the Fox and fell backward with the shock.

'Look where you are going,' said the Fox crossly, and he gave Sam a sharp cuff on his head.

'Very sorry,' said Sam. 'I was taking some important news home.'

'And what is that?' asked the Fox curiously.

'A Circus is coming. A Circus with performing dogs and horses and – and – C for Cabbages,' said Sam hurriedly.

'Indeed. Which night?' asked the Fox.

'Saturday, down in Hemlock Meadow.'

'Ah!' said the Fox. 'Ah! Farmer Greensleeves will doubtless go, and the henplace perhaps – perhaps – '

Then he remembered Sam was listening.

'Yes. What about it?' asked Sam.

'Nothing, only that the henplace will be locked as usual,' remarked the Fox casually, but Sam was sure that wasn't what he had intended to say.

Sam went on his way, running to tell Brock, saying it to himself. 'C for Cabbages. I for Icicle – ' The family was curled up asleep on the rugs and Brock was dozing in his chair when Sam bounded in at the door.

'Brock! Ann! Tom! and Bill! All of you!' he cried, and the little pigs rubbed their eyes and yawned. Here was Sam excited, busy, and talkative when they all wanted to sleep.

'There's a Circus coming to Hemlock Meadow!'

'A Circus? What's that? Why did you wake us?' asked the brothers lazily.

'A Circus?' cried Brock, sitting up wide awake.

'I saw the picture of it on the old door in Hedge-sparrow Lane. There was a red C for Cabbage, and a blue I for Icicle, and a white R for Rain, and another Cabbage, and a Unicorn and and a – a Sam Pig and Sally the Mare.'

'Yes, Circus, Sam. Very good indeed,' said Brock, smiling at the panting, puffing little pigling.

'And a picture of a pretty little girl on a pony, and a

crown on her hair, like Ann at the Maypole, and dogs with frills, and – oh Brock, such a lot of things,' said Sam.

'I must go and see this picture on our door,' said Brock. 'The old auction bill has been there for many months, and I'm glad they've changed it. I must find out about this Circus.'

'Can we go? Can we go to the Circus?' asked all the little pigs at once.

'We'll see,' said Brock, quietly puffing at his pipe. All around the countryside, in many a village and hamlet, children were asking the same question. Mary and Dick Greensleeves were asking their father, 'Can we go? Can we go?' and the blacksmith's daughter was asking her father and the grocer's little boys were asking their father, and the miller's boy was asking the miller, and the parents were replying, 'We'll see,' just like old Brock the Badger.

It seemed as though the family of little pigs couldn't go to the Circus, for when Brock looked in the money-box there was one penny, very old and battered, and a crooked sixpence with a hole bored in it, and a medal that Sam had picked up. The box hadn't been touched for a long time, and a spider had put a fine web all over it.

'How I wish I had kept a bit of that hundred pounds reward for finding the treasure,' said Sam.

'Perhaps we could walk in without paying,' suggested Ann, brightly. 'We went to the Flower Show and nobody stopped us.'

'They might think we were performing pigs,' said Bill.

'I shall go and hunt for a penny in the lanes,' said Sam.

'I'm a good spier, and sometimes there's a penny lost by somebody on the way to market.'

'You won't find enough money to take you to the Circus,' warned Brock. 'I'm afraid we must be content with looking at the outside and listening to the music from a distance.'

Sam Pig hunted and peeped in the flowery hedge bottom where sometimes a penny falls, but all he found was a dirty old halfpenny, lost by a tramp a year ago. He washed it clean and put it in his pocket.

'If only they'd take Pig-money,' said Sam aloud. 'If only they'd take Penny-cress, and Penny-royal, and Penny-wort, then we could all go.'

'They won't, Sam,' said a throstle in the hedge. 'They like silver and copper that nobody can eat.'

At the farm the children were excited with the news of the Circus, and the rumours of its loveliness. They talked of it from morning till night. They were all going, except old Adam, who was staying to keep house while they were away. Even Mollie the dairymaid was invited by her young man.

Sally the Mare talked to Sam Pig about it. 'All of us, on Saturday night,' said she proudly.

Sam looked wistfully at Sally.

'I wish we were going. I do want to see a Circus. You are a lucky mare, Sally.'

'I'm not going *inside* the Circus,' said Sally, opening wide her eyes and shaking her head at the impetuous little pig. 'Nay, Sam lad, they don't let cart-horses go *inside* the Circus tent. I shall wait at the Blue Boar, and have a chat with the horses in the stable there. I'm not going inside the show. Life's enough of a Circus without that, what with ducks on their heads in ponds, and that young colt galloping wild in the fields, and the cows pushing first to be milked, and hens chattering all day, not counting the antics of the pigs. Life's enough of a Circus for me.'

Sam sighed and kicked a stone with his toe.

'All the same, I want to go,' said he to the ground.

'Why don't you?' asked Sally.

'Because it costs money, and our money-box is nearly empty,' said Sam, simply. 'That's why.'

'I'm certain sure Farmer Greensleeves would pay for you,' said Sally. 'He got some money out of the bank only yesterday. You're only little ones, you could sit low down.'

'Do you really think he would?' asked Sam.

'I bet he would,' said Sally, nodding her great head. 'He was saying to the Missis how well you gathered the stones from the fields. Much better than the miller's boy. He said he would like to do something for you, give you a bag of apples or cabbages. I should write to him, Sam. You do that, Sam.'

'I can't write a letter,' said Sam.

'Not write a letter? Why, I thought you were a scholar! I thought you'd been to school!' Sally nearly stepped on Sam, she was so much astonished.

'Only for one day, Sally.'

'And you didn't learn to write letters? No Reading and Writing and Sums? No French and Jogfy and t'other things?'

'No, Sally,' said Sam in a very little voice.

'Why, Sam Pig, I'm ashamed of you,' said Sally.

Sam's ears drooped, and he bent his head to hide a tear.

'I didn't learn nuffin 'scept A for – for Apple, and then Brock said it was A for Ann.'

'Well, well,' said Sally, staring solemnly at the sad little pig. 'Well, write that, Sam. Write A for Ann.'

Sam went away and he began to write letters to Farmer Greensleeves. They were all the same. They lay on paths, in the grass, by walls, on doors, under gates, and wherever Sam could get room for his crooked little letters.

He picked up sticks and framed them into letters as Brock had showed him.

'C for Cabbage,' said he, and he made the letter C in the dust of the farmyard early in the morning when everyone was asleep.

'I for Icicle,' said he, and he added that nice easy letter.

'R for Rain,' said Sam, and he had a fine struggle with that awkward letter.

'C for another Cabbage,' said Sam, and he put a second curved C on the ground next to the R.

'U for Unicorn,' said Sam, and he twisted a slip of willow into a letter U.

'S for Sam and Sally,' cried Sam triumphantly, as he curled and bent the snakelike letter S.

He stood upright and regarded his work. CIRCUS was written in fine strong sticks, of willow and hazel, clear for anyone to read, if the cows didn't walk upon it.

Sam strutted off, very proud, and then he began again in another place. So he went on, writing his solitary word, sending his message with sticks and stones, and moss and seeds. He made it with dandelions and daisies, with nut leaves and snail shells. He wrote it with green rushes, and yellow straw and sweet hay. He used a chalky stone and made the crooked word on the barn door. He even wrote CIRCUS at the front door of the farm, using white pebbles on the doorsill. For hours he worked, at dawn and after dusk, and the word CIRCUS was planted everywhere about the farmhouse and cart roads.

Farmer Greensleeves scratched his head when he saw these queer twisted letters sprinkled over the ground.

'Who's been writing Circus all over the place?' he asked. 'Who's been putting sticks and stones in a litter everywhere? It's main bad writing, whoever did it. Must be somebody playing a trick. What does it mean, this Circus in the yard and down the lane?'

Nobody knew, and when little Dick and Mary Greensleeves came running to say they had found the mysterious word by the pig-cote and in the cow-house, they were quite puzzled.

They kept watch, and in the early dawn just before milking-time, Farmer Greensleeves saw little Sam Pig kneeling in the stackyard laboriously making his crooked word with bits of rope.

'Sam Pig? What's to do? What's all this about Circus?' asked the Farmer.

Sam leapt to his feet, startled at the voice.

'Please, Master, I did it, Master,' he stammered.

'Do you want to go to the Circus, Sam? Is that it?' asked Farmer Greensleeves kindly.

Sam nodded his head violently, not daring to speak.

'Well, I'll take you, Sam.'

'Oh, thank you, Master! Thank you! And Bill and Tom and Ann and Brock the Badger?'

'Yes, the whole caboodle of you. We are going and you shall go too. I've never taken a menagerie to a Circus, but I'll do it. You'll have to walk there, but I'll pay for you and see you through the turnstile, unless they won't admit you.'

'Oh, Master!' said Sam, smiling with an angelic smile.

'And mind you dress yourselves neat and tidy. I don't want to have folk talking,' added the Farmer. 'You meet me outside the Circus, at six o'clock. You'll see us all coming in.'

'Yes, Master, and you'll see us too,' said Sam, gleefully.

'I bet I shall,' said the Farmer softly, and he went indoors to break the news to his wife.

'The whole caboodle of them,' said he again. 'The whole truck-load.'

Then he popped his head outside the kitchen door.

'Sam! No more writing Circus! I've seen that word enough for a lifetime,' said he, shaking his fist.

Sam grinned and ran into the stable to whisper to Sally.

'Sally! We're going. He's taking us. Oh, Sally!'

'I'm proud of you, Sam,' said Sally. 'You are a scholar after all. You did learn something at school.'

Sam went home, turning cart-wheels, swinging on gates, cheering and shouting till he had roused the woodland and scared the rabbits and annoyed the Fox who was waiting to ambush them.

'Sam Pig, you are a foolish young pigling,' said he.

'Oh, Master Fox! I am a scholar, I am,' said Sam.

The family was filled with joy when Sam brought the good news, and Brock patted Sam's head.

'We must all behave well, and be a credit to the farm. Never before has this family gone like royalty to a show,' said Brock. 'We've always had to creep through back doors and here we are going like kings and a queen.'

The next day was Saturday and most of the time was

spent in getting clean and getting dirty and starting all over again. Sam's trousers had been washed the night before by Sister Ann. The pattern of checks in red and blue came clear again when the dirt of a hundred days rolling in the mud was scrubbed away. They hung on the line to dry and Sam lay in bed waiting for them. Little Ann washed her own short skirt, and Brock brushed his coat and trousers. He found new feathers for hats and flowers for buttonholes, and handkerchiefs for pockets. He cut good smooth hazel sticks for the little pigs to carry like all good country-folk.

They had a big tea, and then it was time to start. Brock wore his silver watch, and Ann had her walnut-shell locket dangling round her slim neck.

'No falling in ditches, Sam, no chasing butterflies or fishing for trout, or climbing trees,' said Brock.

They locked the house and hid the key under the stone. Then off they went, chattering softly, squealing with tiny squeaks of glee, whistling and calling to the throstles and blackbirds and the proud cock pheasant, telling them where they were going.

Suddenly Sam stopped.

'Brock! I must go to the farm. I believe the Fox is going to rob the henroost tonight. I must warn them,' said he.

'All right. We'll wait here, and you can nip across the fields,' said Brock.

Sam raced under the hedges and over the ditches, back to the farm. He panted into the farmyard, and there was the cart all ready with the farmer and the children in their Sunday best, and Sally all decked out with her horse-brasses, and the best whip with a blue ribbon tied on it.

'Come along, wife,' called the Farmer. 'It's time we started.' Then he saw little Sam, all bedraggled and tousled, puffing at the gate.

'Hello? What's this? Aren't you going to the Circus?' he asked.

'Please, Master, have you 'membered to double lock the henplace?' asked Sam.

'I haven't,' cried the Farmer, slapping his hand on his pocket. 'I forgot.'

'Fox will be about tonight,' whispered Sam.

'Thank ye kindly, Sam Pig,' said the Farmer, and he got down from his seat and went to the henplace.

Sam was starting off again, when the Farmer called him back.

'I'll give you a lift part way till you catch up with the others,' he offered.

Mrs Greensleeves came out, dressed in her Sunday coat and skirt, and her Sunday hat. She was rather surprised when she saw Sam Pig and she gave a sigh.

'Sam's coming with us,' said Farmer Greensleeves. 'He can ride at the back with the childer.'

So away they went, and the two little children made room for Sam Pig at the back of the cart. When they reached the cross-road, Sam leapt down.

'We shall be there to meet you,' said he.

'You'll go the short cut over the hills, Sam, but I must drive round the valleys. You'll be first I reckon,' said the Farmer.

Sam washed in the stream, and Brock brushed him with a handful of gorse, and Ann rubbed the spots of mud from his trousers. When the little pig was respectable again they went on their way over the hills, through the woods and high places, but far below they could see the white winding road running in and out of the folds of the green hills. Then they saw a glow of lights in the valley, and a cloud of smoke. They could hear the sound of music, and drums, and cries of a happy crowd of people.

'I'm glad we are meeting the Farmer,' said Ann. 'I should be frightened to go there all alone.'

They dropped over the crest of the hill and ran down the green grassy slopes to the river. In Hemlock Meadow stood a great white tent, with a flag waving on the top, and many caravans and booths around it.

Crowds of people were walking about, falling over the tent pegs, staring at the caravans, gazing at the horses tethered in the field, watching the men carry water from the river for the beasts. The family of little pigs went quietly among them, not speaking a word, keeping very close to Brock who looked like a little old countryman, as he smoked his pipe. They were all very much excited with the smells of strange animals, the sounds of foreign voices, and the bewildering sights. Dogs barked and horses whinnied, and clowns looked out of tent doorways. They got glimpses of gilded saddles and white-powdered faces, of clowns and beautiful piebald ponies. The band played inside the great tent, and a fine gentleman shouted at the entrance, asking the people to come in. A lady blazing with jewels took the money as the crowd slowly wended its way through the sacking corridor.

The little family stood on one side, trying not to be swept along with the others.

'Seems as if some of the Circus has escaped,' said a woman, pointing to Sam Pig.

'Performing pigs, they is,' said another.

'Put out here for advertisement,' said a third, and she gave Sam a poke with her umbrella.

There was a bustle and commotion, and stout Farmer Greensleeves pushed his way through with Mrs Greensleeves and the children.

'Here we are, Master,' squeaked Sam.

'Come along. Follow me and the Missis, next to us, with the children last. Dick and Mary, you go after this lot,' said the Farmer, hurriedly collecting them in a bunch.

They joined in the procession, and squeezed together very close, trying to make themselves as small as possible.

'Two half-crowns and two at half-price for the children and five seats at threepence for – for – for the rest of us,' said the Farmer, taking his money-bag out of his pocket.

The jewelled woman peered over to see who was passing so low down, for the little pigs were nearly out of sight.

'Dwarfs,' she muttered. 'Midgets,' said she. 'Midgets, threepence each.'

'That's right,' said the Farmer. 'Midgets, threepence each.'

So they all walked into the Great Top, which is the Circus tent. The little family parted from the farmer, who went to the red baize-covered seats. The four little pigs and old Brock sat on the front row far away from the others, on a low wooden plank, and with them sat the poorest children, and a few farm boys. It was really the best seat of all.

They had a beautiful view of everything, and their short legs rested comfortably on the green turf. It is true that nobody bowed to them, and the ring-master was facing the other way, but that made it all the better.

They saw the blacked feet of the sparkling piebald ponies, and they could nearly touch the scarlet bridles and gold tassels. The horses' hooves thundered close to them but they had no fear. The clowns took no notice of them, they were too busy telling their jokes to the rich people at the other side of the Circus, and so the four pigs could tell their own little jokes to a small pony who came close to them.

'Hello,' said Sam, in a soft animal whisper. 'Would you like a lump of sugar?'

'Yes, please,' said the little pony, pushing its nose to Sam's pocket. Sam brought out a fistful of sugar and the pony feasted.

'Who are you?' asked the pony.

'Sam Pig and family, all come to the Circus,' whispered Sam.

'And I am Pepper the Pony,' said the small pony, frisking and dancing on its hind legs to show Sam what it could do.

The ring-master saw there was something going on in that remote corner, and he cracked his whip. Away ran little Pepper, to gallop round the circle, and tell everyone that Sam Pig and family had come to the Circus.

After that every animal stopped near Sam and Brock for a word or two, for a grunt or a squeak of recognition.

Clowns tumbled about the ring, and the laughter of the four little pigs rang out, higher than any other. Here was something they understood – rolling and playing and teasing. The clowns glanced towards these merrymakers, and one of them came up, and held out his pointed hat in mockery. Sam took it and put it on. Then he handed it back and the puzzled clown bowed to him.

'That's good,' said the people. 'They've got a pigling sitting down on the front row, trained to wear a hat.'

'See me afterwards,' muttered the clown to Sam.

'Behave yourself, Sam,' grumbled Brock. 'Don't shame Farmer Greensleeves. We haven't come here to see your tricks.'

Sam was abashed. He sat very still and quiet, but when a beautiful young girl with gold hair and a wreath of flowers came riding in, he sat up and smiled.

Round and round she went, bowing to the people, and when she passed Sam she bowed to him too. Then she stood on the pony's back and danced lightly on one toe, while the animal galloped gently round the ring. The clown held out a paper hoop. Like a fairy she leapt through it, tearing the thin paper, and alighting on the broad back of her pony. Other clowns ran in with blue and yellow hoops of paper, and the girl danced through them all, leaving streamers like ribbons behind her. Sam leapt up in his seat. He grabbed a hoop from one of the clowns and held it high, dipping it as the pony ambled towards him.

'Jump,' he cried, and the girl leapt through it, but the pony was so startled by Sam's squeak, it swerved, and only just caught the girl in time.

Brock seized Sam by the trousers and hauled him back to the seat. Ann was jigging up and down, Tom and Bill were clapping like mad.

Farmer Greensleeves was looking at them. He shook his head and laughed.

'Those pigs are enjoying themselves and no mistake,' he observed to his wife.

Next came the jugglers, who threw up cups and balls and bottles and caught them. 'Brock is a far better juggler than these men,' thought Sam. Clever Brock who could outwit the Leprechaun, and tease a fairy, was quicker with hand and eye than any human juggler.

A trapeze artist hung from the roof, and swung from ropes and ladders, as if he were in the branches of a high tree. He flung himself down and caught a swing half-way. Then came a dazzling display, as he leapt through the air, and swung by toes and fingers.

'He's like a squirrel,' said Ann Pig, staring up at the slim lithe man. 'I never knew man was like a squirrel before.'

'Man is like everything,' said Brock solemnly. 'He can swim in the sea and fly in the air. That's why he is dangerous.'

The little dogs came running in, excitedly barking, shaking the frills which decked their bodies, tossing their heads with the pointed hats. How the children laughed and shouted, and how the little pigs squeaked as they saw them! The dogs held up their paws and walked on their hind legs, they danced and smoked pipes and balanced on rolling barrels.

Sam bobbed about excitedly, and there was a sudden crack! He jigged again, and there was a crash! Down went the wooden form, and children and piglings and Brock all were thrown to the floor.

'Now see what you've done,' grumbled Bill Pig, scrambling out of the broken pieces. 'Upset us when we were comfortable.'

Everybody was laughing at the little legs in the air, and the squeals and cries as they rolled over together.

'Some people are enjoying themselves,' said a clown loudly. 'Doing circus tricks on their own.'

He ran up with a feather brush and tickled their faces, and set them in a row on the grass.

Next came a strange animal with no legs, who flip-flopped across the grass, and raised itself with flippers on a barrel.

'What is it?' asked Sam. 'Is it a kind of mermaid?'

'It's a seal,' whispered Brock the Badger.

The seal's sharp ears heard the animal voices and it turned its head towards the four little pigs.

'Solomon Seal, from the Ocean,' it said in a deep gruff voice, and it barked huskily and grunted like an old sow.

The keeper gave it fish, and it clapped its flippers, and said, 'Solomon Seal. Solomon,' but of course only the pigs understood its language.

Then the man threw a ball to it, and it tossed it up, playing cleverly, balancing the ball on its nose. Sam Pig crept from his seat, and sidled away towards the seal. 'Catch,' barked the seal. Sam caught the ball and tossed it back, and then began a game of catch between Sam Pig and the seal.

The keeper stood aside, staring in astonishment, but Sam never dropped the ball, and the seal played with it and threw it to the little pig, and caught it again, so rapidly that everyone stood up and clapped.

Sam bowed and the seal clapped its flippers, and the keeper slapped Sam on the back.

'See me afterwards,' said he.

'Behave yourself,' muttered Brock crossly, as Sam ran

back to his seat. 'You are disgracing the family by your bold antics, Sam. What will Farmer Greensleeves say? What's the matter with you?'

Sam sat on the grass, half hidden, but his eyes were shining, and he was breathing quickly with the excitement of the ring.

So the Circus display went on, with new delights every minute. Then came the great scene, when Fairy Bell, sitting in her little gold chariot, drove six diminutive grey ponies into the ring. The big black horses paced round with necks arched and legs high-lifted, and among them went the tiny carriage with the small girl driving her team.

Everybody clapped, but Sam Pig, Ann Pig, Bill and Tom with Brock the Badger clapped their hands and stamped their hooves with excitement. Little Sam clapped so hard and so long that the clown who had been watching him suddenly picked him up and popped him in the carriage by Fairy Bell's side. Such a roar of cheering went up! Sam was frightened for a moment, and then he smiled and waved, and the little Fairy Bell smiled and bowed too.

'Beauty and the Beast,' called the clown. 'Fairy Bell has now met Prince Charming.'

Everybody laughed, for Sam's ears stuck out, his hat was awry, and his little face was dirty. He didn't mind, and Fairy Bell was happy enough. Sometimes one of the dogs rode by her side, and now she had a small pigling for companion.

'Gee up! Gee up!' called Sam to the six little ponies, and when they heard Sam's voice they galloped quite fast. Brock the Badger sat in his seat, feeling rather anxious about Sam. He thought this was a kidnapping act and Sam was stolen away by the Circus people. He frowned and muttered to himself something about conceited piglings who have no sense, but Sam was smiling and waving and laughing in the little gold carriage, by the side of the charming young Fairy Bell.

When the ponies started for the doorway, Sam stood up.

'Good-bye, Fairy Bell,' said he, and he kissed the little girl and leapt down, just as if he were climbing from the farmer's cart. Then away he ran, padding very fast across the ring, and over the wooden border to the family.

The people cheered, again and again. It was all part of the fun of the Circus, and they thought it was the best act of all.

The band played God Save the Queen, Sam stood up with everyone else, and Brock the Badger was stiff, with hair all bristled as if he would fight all the queen's enemies. Sam could hear Brock growling and he thought the Badger was singing but in reality Brock was feeling very angry indeed.

'Do you want to join us? Circus life will suit you,' said the clown, running across and speaking to Sam. 'The manager will see you now. Follow me. You've got just the face for a Circus success.'

Sam hesitated a moment, for he could hear those growls like low thunder. Circus life would be beautiful, and he longed to ride again in the chariot with Fairy Bell, but there was Sally the Mare. He didn't want to leave Sally.

'Well,' said he slowly. 'It's very kind of you, and I should like to ride every night in Fairy Bell's little cart, and I can look after the ponies, but I know a big cart-horse called Sally the Mare, and if she can come too –'

'She can. Yes, she can,' said the clown.

Brock the Badger was growling like a lion. His deep growl grew louder, he snarled, and bared his teeth. The clown took a quick step backward, when he heard that horrid noise.

'Sam Pig! Come away home. No more nonsense,' said Brock in an angry voice, and he gave Sam a sharp nip. Sam didn't wait to say any more. Neither did the clown. He went back double-quick to the Circus folk to tell of the queer things he had seen and heard. Sam meekly followed the family out of the tent into the cold starlit night.

The fresh air brought him to his senses. They walked home across the hills, a little band wandering in the shadowed by-ways, unseen by any after their brief and exciting appearance in society. They chattered about the Circus all the way, but Sam was quiet. The others tried the tricks as they ran along the paths, they swung on the branch of an overhanging tree, and danced and galloped. They repeated the clown's jokes, and rolled over one another.

It wasn't till they reached home that Brock spoke to Sam.

'Why did you think of going with that clown?' asked Brock sternly.

'I thought it would be nice to be in a Circus,' faltered Sam. 'I should like to look after six ponies and Fairy Bell.'

'It isn't all riding in chariots, Sam. It's a hard life, and you are a lazy little fellow. Remember what happened when man stole you, long ago. Man's a hard task-master, little Sam. Besides, we can't do without our Sam Pig.'

'No,' whispered Sam. 'I won't go.'

For weeks the little pig family played at Circus. They made a tight-rope out of the washing-line, and tried to balance on it. They put frills round their necks and danced like the dogs. They skipped and pranced and turned somersaults, like the clowns. Sam even rode on Sally's back, and tried to leap through a hoop of twisted hazel that Ann Pig held out. Of course he caught his foot in it, and fell headlong, but he got up quickly and tried again.

'I sometimes wish I had gone, Sally,' confided Sam in the mare's ear. 'I might have been riding in a golden chariot now, by the side of the beautiful Fairy Bell.'

'And you might be scrubbing out an old caravan, and nobody caring a button about you,' said Sally. 'You be content and stay where you are wanted, Sam Pig. That Fox didn't get into the henroost. You stay here, Sam.'

'Yes,' said Sam meekly. 'Yes, Sally.'

The Little Fiddler

(Written to the music of *The Little Fiddler*, by Nechaiev)

LITTLE IVAN stood at the door of his home in the square of a small Russian town. The travelling players had come, and he watched them unpack their chairs, their tables and cooking-pots, and set them out under the trees. They lighted a fire and cooked a meal, all the time laughing and talking in high spirits. Children wandered among them, asking questions, but Ivan was too shy to join the others. He waited with one hand on the wooden latch of his kitchen door, hesitating, longing to go near but half afraid.

'Aren't you going to look at the players, Ivan?' called his mother from the stove. 'Why don't you run across the square?'

Slowly Ivan walked away, but when he got near he stood in the shadows by the little scarlet cart which held the furniture and properties. One of the showmen came to the cart, and rummaged among the blankets. He brought out a fiddle, and he tuned it, there in the firelight. Ivan watched with great wondering eyes. Pots were simmering, children shouting, and the fiddle gave little grunts and wails as the man tightened the pegs and held it lovingly. Ivan caught his breath as the man played a few notes. The light flashed on the dark skin of the fiddler, tanned to the colour of the violin, and the music spoke to Ivan.

Suddenly the man swung round, the fiddle under his chin, his bow still sighing over the strings, bringing lovely notes into the air. He looked hard at Ivan, a little boy half-hidden by the cart-wheels.

'Well?' he asked. 'What do you want, great-eyes?'

'Comrade,' stammered Ivan. 'I want a fiddle, just a little one.'

'You want a little one, do you?' echoed the man. He grabbed Ivan's shoulder and drew him to the light, regarding him keenly.

'If you like to join my company of players for two years, I'll give you a fiddle and teach you to play it. I want a boy to look after the horses and to do the odd jobs.'

'I'll come,' said Ivan, without hesitation.

'Where do you live?' asked the showman.

'Over there. My father is a woodcutter.'

'Go and ask his permission first. I take no boy who isn't free to travel, and willing to learn.'

So Ivan ran home and asked his mother and father if he could go for two years with the travelling players.

At first they said no, but later they went to the square to watch the company act and play by firelight and torch-light. There, on the beaten earth, the little group of men and women acted a fairy play about the Old Witch Woman; they danced, dressed in brightly coloured trousers, flashing with gold; they played tambourines, and beat drums; they juggled with knives and they sang barbaric, stirring songs. The fiddler, whose name was Nicholas, stood near, playing his tunes, and all the time he played there was some magic about. Even the stars in the sky twinkled red and green, and the moon remained over the old apple tree a full hour without moving at all. An owl sat in the branches, unwinking, with round eyes staring, astonished, and Ivan stared too.

'They are good players, they are artists,' said Ivan's father, slowly twisting his beard and glancing at his son.

'Can I go with them?' asked Ivan urgently. 'Can I?'

'What does your mother say?' said his father. 'She's the law-giver. She must decide.'

Marie took the boy's hot hand in hers and gave it a squeeze.

'Do you want to go very much?' she asked.

He nodded and whispered, 'Yes, Mother.'

'Then you shall. They are real artists. But you must promise to do your best and learn all you can, and come back to us in two years.'

So the next day when the company had packed their tents and cooking-pots on the backs of the horses and in the scarlet cart, Ivan joined them.

It was a hard life for the boy, for he was everybody's servant. It was 'Ivan, catch the horses. Ivan, gather some firewood. Ivan, mind the pot. Look after the babies. Collect the money. Fill the water buckets,' all day and half the night. Often he wished he was safe at home, and twice he made up his mind to run away, but each time he was stopped by the enchanting music of the fiddle. When the leader played, everything was forgotten. All hardships vanished, bruises stopped aching, his sore feet were refreshed, his tired eyes were bright again.

'It goes to your heart, little one, does it?' said Nicholas the fiddler, staring down at the boy one day as he sat on an upturned basket, listening.

'It makes me feel different,' said Ivan slowly. 'Look, there were sores on my feet, and they've gone. I had a pain in my head yesterday when Peter the Driver thrashed me, but the pain went when you played your fiddle. Why is it?'

'You're made that way. My fiddle doesn't cure Peter's bad temper, or old Anna's sharp tongue,' said Nicholas bitterly.

'When can I have that little fiddle you promised me?' asked Ivan.

'Soon, my child. I've been watching you, and you shall have it before the new moon comes up the sky. I must make it from wood cut from a silver birch when the moon is full. I must carry the wood till the moon wanes, and then make the fiddle as the new moon waxes great. That is the way to fashion a little fiddle for a boy.'

When the moon was full, Nicholas the fiddler went to the forest and cut down a silver birch, with the light falling upon it. He carried small pieces of the wood with him, and one night, when the new moon shone like a silver arc in the blue sky, he carved a little fiddle. It was a clumsy little thing, heavy, square cut, but it was a real fiddle, made from seventy-four strips of birch.

He fitted the four strings of catgut and the pegs to tune them and the little bridge of strange delicacy. There was a letter carved in that bridge, the letter O, the symbol of eternity. Then he made a bow for Ivan, with hair from the long tail of the white horse and a tip cut from box-wood.

'Will this fiddle you're making really play?' asked Peter the Driver, as Nicholas carved the tail in an up-turned sweep. 'I will buy it from you, Nicholas.'

'Not for you,' replied Nicholas, abruptly. 'It will only shriek like a pig if you touch it, Peter. It is Ivan's, something he has worked for, and he will be able to get tunes from it, you'll see.'

Peter stamped off, scowling, but Ivan came closer to his friend, and bent over to watch Nicholas's fingers at work.

As usual in the evening the party gave their performance of dance and song and music. Ivan collected the money and hobbled the horses and set the tents up for the night.

When the performance was over, and the boy's eyes were closing with tiredness, and his body was reeling about with desire for sleep, Nicholas came over to him. He held out the tiny fiddle, polished with a secret varnish, sweet-smelling of the birch trees.

'Ivan, your fiddle is ready. Keep it close to you. Good night.'

Ivan's weary fingers clutched the instrument. He stumbled on his heap of straw under the body of the cart, and fell asleep with the fiddle pressed to his heart. Somebody kicked him in passing, but he only curled up closer and held the treasure more tightly. Once in the night he awoke, opened wide his eyes and gazed at it. The moon was looking down at him, and a finger of light silvered that little piece of birch-wood and touched the strings. A strange musical sound came from it, and everything stirred to listen. The horses whinnied, a wild swan flew over, and murmurs and rustles were all around. Then Ivan slept again.

The next day he was up at cockcrow. Nicholas was already starting to pack the wagon, and Peter was shouting. The horses had to be fetched from the field where they had spent the night, water was carried from the stream, and all was bustle and preparation for the move onward.

Ivan ran here and there, with the fiddle slung round his neck. While the others were eating their rye bread and drinking coffee, he slipped away to the wood and tuned his fiddle, as he had seen Nicholas tune his. He drew the bow across the strings, uncertain and trembling. The most enchanting thin notes came out, clear as water. Fiddle-de-dee. Fiddle-de-dee. Fiddle-de-dee.

There was a rustle of wings, and a big black crow flew down. A rabbit came from its burrow. A great wolf looked through the clearing, and sat there on its haunches, with red rongue lolling. Ivan saw it, from the corner of his eye. He backed slowly away, still playing his wavering first tune, and the wolf left him in peace.

'Ivan. Ivan,' a shout rang through the wood, and he hurried back to the actors.

'Well, little one, do you like your fiddle?' asked Nicholas, smiling.

'Yes, indeed I do. I can play a tune, Nicholas. I played, and a tune came out.'

'Well, you shall play it to me, and if I like it, you shall perform tonight with us, Ivan. No longer are you the servant here. I have promoted you. Comrades all! Let me introduce you to a new member of our profession. Ivan the Little Fiddler,' he called to the others.

'Ivan the Little Fiddler,' they shouted and cheered. All except Peter the Driver.

'Who's going to fetch the horses and harness them, and carry water and chop wood if young Ivan is to be a fiddler?' he demanded.

'You, of course,' said Nicholas sternly. 'You, Peter.'

Then began days and nights of delight for young Ivan. He was dressed in scarlet silk trousers, and short green jacket, with gold buttons and tassels. He wore a gold-braided scarlet cap on his fair hair. He came to the centre of the ring, and stood in the firelight, under the night sky, and played his little fiddle to the village audiences. They cheered the boy, and he played again, something gay and merry. Everybody liked his music, for he brought tunes out of the air, lingering there, little dancing tunes which must have been waiting for many years for somebody to find them.

Every night, when the music was done, and the people had gone home, he lay down in a corner of the tent near Nicholas. His gay clothes were folded and packed away in the cart, but the fiddle was in his arms. Each afternoon, as they travelled on, or rested for a time, Nicholas gave Ivan lessons, and showed him better fingering, and cleaner touch.

One day as the company of players went along the road they saw a white chicken caught in the brambles. Peter the Driver darted forward, and was going to wring its neck, for he wanted something for the stew-pot. The chicken cried out in fear, and Ivan heard it. He ran up, playing his little fiddle.

'Oh, let it alone, Peter. It is only a chicken, Peter.'

'Why should I?' grunted Peter, but his hand was stayed and the chicken escaped, crying 'Ivan. Ivan has saved me.'

Ivan went on playing, and the chicken sang to the tune.

'Fiddle-de-dee
Ivan has saved me.
A chicken so small,
No size at all,
If he's afraid,
I'll come to his aid.'

How Ivan laughed, but he played his gay tune, and the chicken sang till the cavalcade was out of sight.

Another day the company of players saw a calf tied up to a tree waiting for the butcher. Poor little thing, it was blorting sadly for its mother. Ivan, playing his fiddle, went to the farmer.

'Save the little cow-calf,' said he. 'It's only young. I'll give you all my money for its life.'

'Let me see your money,' said the farmer.

Ivan had only a few roubles, but he held them out and then went on playing.

'The money's not much, but I'll do as you wish,' said the farmer. 'I'll keep the calf and let it grow to be a cow, if you'll play that tune again to me.'

Then the calf was freed, and it ran swiftly to its mother. As it went, Ivan could hear the words it called.

'Fiddle-de-dee
Ivan has saved me,
To stay with my mother.
Then I and no other

Will go to his aid,
If he is afraid.'

On they went, playing, singing, acting their fairy play, and Ivan gave his own performance every night at a fresh village.

One evening, as they prepared for the performance, they saw a little cat up a tree, with a fierce dog barking below. The poor little cat was so frightened, it seemed as if it must fall right into the jaws of that savage dog. When Ivan went near, the dog flew at him, but he just managed to play a few bars on his birch-wood fiddle.

The dog stopped still, listening.

'Here is some dinner,' said Ivan, taking a hunk of bread from his pocket. 'Eat this, and leave the little cat alone.'

Away ran the dog, gruzzling and grunting with the bread in its mouth, and the little cat climbed down the tree and purred and rubbed itself against Ivan's legs.

'I'll play you a tune,' said Ivan, and he played a lively air. The cat sang, and the boy heard the words, although nobody else understood.

'Fiddle-de-dee
Ivan has saved me.
I'm only a cat,
No matter for that,
If he is afraid,
I'll come to his aid.'

Another day he saw a bird struggling in the fowler's net. The poor bird was exhausted with fear, but Ivan ran up and set it free. Away it flew to the high bough of a tree, where it sang a triumphal song, promising to aid Ivan.

'Fiddle-de-dee
Ivan has saved me.
I'm a little white bird.
When the fiddle I heard
I knew it was he.
Ivan has saved me.'

A week later Ivan saw a bee caught in a spider's web. It was a fat little bumble bee, with a red-brown waistcoat. It was buzzing in a tiny voice 'Save me, Ivan. Save me, Ivan.'

Ivan played his fiddle, and the web tore apart. The spider hurried off to a chink in the wall, and the little bee flew up in the air, humming with all its might.

'Fiddle-de-dee
Ivan has saved me.
I am only a bee,
But the world shall see,
I may save him,
Who has now saved me.'

That was a cheerful summery song and Ivan called it 'The Song of the Bee'.

The artists were getting famous and they had saved a heap of money which they kept in a locked chest in the scarlet cart. Peter the Driver thought of this store of gold; day and night he longed to get hold of it, but there was no chance. Nicholas and Ivan slept close to the cart, with their tent-door opening to it. Peter plotted with some robbers in the woods and made a plan. He always cooked the meals now, and the robbers gave him some herbs to put in the broth that would make the company sleep very soundly. Nothing would wake them, and the robbers could then join Peter and take the gold.

'This broth has a bitter taste tonight,' said Nicholas. 'What have you put in it? Rue or wormwood?'

'Rue, Nicholas. It is good for your health in the spring weather,' laughed Peter. It was the poisonous henbane he had added to the broth.

'You are not eating and drinking, tonight, Peter. What's the matter?' asked Nicholas.

'I tasted so much of the broth when I was making it, that I had enough. Good cooks always dig their spoons in their dishes,' said Peter.

Now the robbers had arranged a signal to show Peter they were near. It was the cry of an owl. If the company was asleep, then Peter would hoot back to tell them to attack.

This cry rang out: 'Tu whit, Tu whoo.' It was a shrill, moaning cry, just like the wild owl calling to its mate.

'Listen,' said Nicholas, pausing with a spoonful of broth. 'The owls are calling early tonight. Do you reply to them, Ivan. Perhaps we can lure one to our camp fire.'

Ivan took up his little fiddle and played the eldrich 'To whit, Tu whoo,' of one owl answering another.

There was a rustle in the trees, and the robbers came rushing to the camp to seize the company. The players fought desperately, but they were already drowsy with the broth, and the robbers were strong.

Then Ivan played his fiddle, calling for help, sending out his music to the forest. The sound of it went through the air rousing all those birds and animals which had been befriended by the boy. A white hen flew up through the trees, and fell with beak and claw on the robbers in the darkness.

Next came a cow with long horns, followed by a herd of cattle snorting and roaring with anger. The robbers were attacked on every side by the long horns and hard hooves. There was a caterwauling like fifty evil spirits turned loose, and the little white cat came with an army of friends to the rescue. With claws as sharp as daggers the cats fought, and the robbers screamed for mercy, and ran away. A flock of birds flew down and tore their hair. Then came a cloud of bees to sting them. That was the end. The robbers ran till they could run no more. Beaten, tossed, bitten, stung, scratched, they fled, and Peter the Driver went with them.

The little band of players brushed their clothes, set the tents to rights and lifted the chest of gold back to the cart. They hobbled the horses and lay down to sleep after doctoring their cuts and wounds. Near Ivan's tent rested a white cat and a cow, a white bird and a snowy hen, and the little bumble bee, all very tired.

'We will never leave you, Ivan,' they cried, each in his own tongue, with a mew and a moo, a chirrup and a cackle, and a buzz from the bumble bee.

So off they went with the cavalcade next morning, across the plains, with Ivan fiddling to them. They even made a little show of their own, to amuse the next village.

At last the players came to Ivan's own town, and the travelling players unpacked their chairs, their tables and their cooking-pots and set them out under the trees. What rejoicings there were! Ivan's father and mother ran out to welcome their boy and all the children flocked round to question him.

'Wait till night,' said he. 'Then you'll see our play.'

When the stars were out and the moon had risen in a thin bow of gold, the company acted their fairy play of the Old Witch who had feet like a Hen. They danced, dressed in bright colours flashing with gold. They played tambourines and beat drums. They juggled with knives and they sang barbaric, stirring songs, to the music of Nicholas's violin.

Then the little fiddler, who had been standing in the shadows, came forward, bravely clad in scarlet trousers and green jacket, with a rose pinned in the lapel. He played his little birch-wood fiddle in the centre of the ring and from it came such entrancing tunes, they all clapped their hands.

'Bravo. Bravo,' they cried. 'Yes, he is an artist now.'

'Will you come home or stay with the players?' asked his mother, when he had finished, and the people were pushing around him, to touch his gold fringes and stroke his fine coat.

'I must stay with the players now, Mother,' said Ivan. 'This is the life I've chosen. But I have a little company here, who will rest at home and keep you from being lonely.'

He showed them the white cat, the milking-cow, the hen, the bird and the bee, and his mother and father made them very welcome.

So the cat sat on the hearth, the cow went to the byre, the bird flew to the roof-top, the hen went under the table, and the bee lived in a hole in the wall.

'Here we are and here we will stay till Ivan comes home again,' said they. 'We will catch your mice, give you milk and eggs, sing to you and hum to you.'

'You won't be sad while you have these friends, will you?' asked Ivan, and he put his fiddle to his chin and played, which made them all merry. They forgot he was going out into the world again, they were so happy, and it was not till he had left with the players the next morning that they suddenly realized they were alone.

'Fiddle-de-dee,' said the little white cat, and the cow and the hen, the bird and the bee.

'He is a great artist. We have given him to the world,' said the old man and woman, and they went back to the house, contented.

The Crooked Man

In the village of Crick there lived, once upon a time, a homeless boy. Nobody knew where he came from, for one day, after a tribe of gipsies had passed with their dogs and horses, their caravans and carts, a poor little child was found wrapped in a piece of sacking, underneath a gorse-bush. He was brought up in the workhouse, and a more bedraggled twisted little fellow was never seen. He had bandy legs, crooked arms and a humped back. He was christened Thomas Furze, since it was under the furze-blossoms he was found, but the children called him the 'Crooked Lad' or 'Crooked Tom'. Like a broken twig, or a wizened leaf he drifted quietly along the roads, under the hedgerows, up the lanes, seeking what he could find.

When he left the dame's school he had to earn his living, but all he could do was to scare the crows from Farmer Dale's ploughland. So there he sat on the stone walls, or he walked up and down the grassy verges of the fields, swinging his clacker and singing at the top of his shrill voice:

'O! All you little blacky-tops,
Pray don't you eat the farmer's crops.
Shua-O! Shua-O!'

All the crows flew away when they saw him, they were so frightened, for he was more like a living scarecrow than anything else, with his rags flapping and his thin arms waving.

He earned a penny a day for this work, and half a pint of milk, with some broken scraps of food. Now and then he caught a rabbit, or the farmer's wife gave him hot broth and a couple of eggs.

He took all home to the hovel where he lodged, and cooked his supper over his scanty fire. Somehow he managed to live, for his wants were few. He wandered over the meadows, looking for mushrooms and blackberries, for crab-apples and sloes. He found flowers and fruit when other people passed by with unseeing eyes, for his sight was keen as a hawk's. His bright black eye spied the bird on the nest, the tiny field creatures running in the grass, the wild bee flying from its hole. He knew the names of herbs, too, pennycress, bedstraw, and shepherd's-purse, and he could make simples and cures from them, but where he got his knowledge no one knew. Perhaps it was from his roaming ancestors, the gipsies, or he might have watched Old Biddy, the herb-doctor, for whom he sometimes worked. He made balsams and ointments for hurts and wounds, earning a few pence, but he was always poor and lonely.

One day he went up the fields, his sharp eyes as usual

darting here and there, at hedge and ditch and wall. His hands were full of honeysuckle, his pockets brimmed with blackberries and nuts. As he walked his crooked way along the uneven grassy lane, he came to a stile. He wriggled between the tall narrow stones, and on the ground he saw something sparkle. He stooped down and picked up a sixpence, crooked as his own legs. There was a hole through it, where it had hung on somebody's watch-chain.

'A lucky bit!' cried the crooked little man, and he put it between his teeth to see if it was good, and rubbed it on his sleeve to polish it, and peered through the hole at the sun.

'This is the first time I've ever had a real piece of luck! What shall I buy with it?'

He pondered as he went along, and thought of all the things he liked. Dumplings, chitterlings, savoury-puddings, bull's-eyes, all made his mouth water. Or should he buy a tin whistle? The food would go, but the whistle would remain to cheer him when he sat rattling to the crows.

He carried the sixpence a week or two before he decided, and then he bought none of these things. In a cottage in the village lived a little sandy cat, a crooked humpbacked cat, which rubbed itself against his legs in such a friendly manner that he stopped and considered it. He stared at it for a minute or two, and a thought came into his poor tousled head. He stroked the little cat, and the animal purred and pressed close to him, and followed him. He went through the wicket-gate which shut out the garden with its clipped hedge, its neat flower-beds, and the shadowy light of the trees. He touched his cap, and said:

'Will you sell me your kitling, Master? I'll give a sixpenny bit for her, if you'll part with her.'

The man at the door looked at him and at the cat twining herself round his ankles.

'Why, it's Crooked Tom!' he cried. 'You want that poor morsel? You can have her for nowt, and good riddance. We only keep her out of pity.'

'Nay, I want to pay for her, and then she will be mine.' Tom proudly held out his coin, shining and bright with all the polish he had given it.

'Have it your own way,' laughed the man, and Tom went off with the crooked little cat running behind him, purring with all its might. The very first night it caught a mouse in the hovel, so Tom hadn't to provide it with any supper, which was just as well. Then it slept in his arms, and he curled up with the cat's warm fur against his cheek. He was glad he had bought the kitling instead of dumplings or whistles, he thought, as he felt the small heart throbbing, and the creature quivering with happiness and friendliness.

Months went by, and the crooked little man followed by his crooked little cat was a familiar sight. They explored fresh fields together, and wandered miles along the roads and overgrown lanes, always bringing back something new. Sometimes Tom took a basket of red crabs, or a capful of mushrooms to Mrs Dale, the farmer's wife. Sometimes he twisted a hazel switch into a bow, and made arrows hardened in the fire and shafted with goose feathers for the farmer's little boy, or wove little green baskets of rushes for the young girl. He did all these things without thought of reward, just for the pleasure of speaking to human beings, or to get a glimpse of the kitchen fire, and a smell of the roast in the oven. All the time the crooked little cat grew, for the sunshine and exercise made her strong, and there was plenty of wild food for her. She became a splendid animal, fierce and strong as a small yellow tiger, with great eyes and thick golden fur.

Now the barns and cart-sheds and stables were overrun with rats, and Farmer Dale was troubled about his grain and corn which disappeared as if an army were carrying it away. Holes appeared in bins and sacks, and trickles of oats and wheat lay on the floor.

'I'm fair mithered about the rats,' said he, mournfully. 'I've tried poison, and ferrets, cats, dogs and guns, but nothing keeps them down.'

'The crooked man has a fine cat,' said Mrs Dale. 'I should think it is a good ratter.'

'I'll ask him about it,' replied the farmer, and he went out to the fields, where Tom sat on a stone roller, waving his wooden clacker.

'She's a grand ratter,' cried Tom, when he heard the farmer's request, 'and I'd lend her to you with pleasure, but she won't stay anywhere without me.' The great humped cat rubbed herself against his legs, and stared with her odd green and gold eyes at Mr Dale. 'I'll sleep in the barn,' Tom continued. 'It's a deal warmer than my own place, and the straw's a better bed, and cleaner, too.'

So into the barn he went, and slept soundly, heedless of the scattering and scampering and rioting which went on around him, but the next morning a pile of dead rats and mice told of the crooked cat's work. From barn to stable he went, and slept by the manger, from stable to cow-house, from cow-house to cart-shed, and always the rats were cleared by the clever crooked cat.

'It's a grand life,' exclaimed Tom, 'to sleep with warm animals around you, and a good roof overhead, and a bowl of bread and milk for supper!'

The time came for him to return to his hovel, and he put his belongings into a small bundle and started off home. The farm was cleared of its vermin, and he had some shillings in his pocket.

Mrs Dale watched him go, and then she turned to her husband. 'The crooked man is a good-hearted creature,' she said, 'kind to the children, good to the beasts, and knowledgeable with herbs. His cat has done us a good turn.'

'It's a champion cat, although it's crooked,' replied the farmer, 'and he's a likeable fellow, although his wits wander.'

'He has no home,' continued kindly Mrs Dale, 'nothing but that dirty hovel where he lodges. Couldn't he live in our empty cottage?'

'In that twisty old cot!' exclaimed her husband. 'Well, nobody lives there, except hens and ducks. I could make room for them somewhere else. Yes, if you like, missis, he shall have the shepherd's old cot.'

'Let it be a secret,' cried the children, when they heard the news. 'Let us make it all nice for him! Let us give him a big surprise!'

So they took buckets and brooms and whitewash, and soap and dusters and paintpots, and went to the tiny house, with its crooked oak timbers, its bent chimney, its deeply dipping thatch. The thatcher mended the roof with fresh yellow straw. Molly the milkmaid cleaned the house, and Mrs Dale whitewashed the walls. The little boy put a coat of green paint on the dingy woodwork, and the little girl beeswaxed the twisted oak staircase. The windows were mended, the rafters were brushed, and in the inglenook a great fire was lighted to air the kitchen. The floor was stoned with sand, the narrow garden path was weeded and swept, and a pile of firewood was left leaning against the side of the cottage.

Then Mrs Dale looked in her attic at the farm, and brought out a crooked little rocking chair, a twisty table, and a bed which was grand when its lost leg was replaced by a block of wood. The little girl collected old blankets, and the little boy took a frying-pan, a mug and a kettle. On the window-sill they set a scarlet geranium, and at the windows they hung blue curtains, faded to the colour of pale forget-me-nots, which they had found in their grandmother's ancient leather trunk.

Then they called the crooked man, who was starting off home after his work was done. He came round to the back door of the farm, his cap in his hand, his back bent, and his legs wobbling, whilst behind him stood the crooked sandy cat. He waited in the yard by the sycamore tree, tired as he thought of the long trudge to his hovel, and the miserable room awaiting him there.

Out came Mrs Dale and her children, carrying baskets covered with white cloths.

'We have something to show you, Tom. We hope you are not too tired to come with us across the pastures.'

'No, Ma'am, I'll come with pleasure,' replied the little man. They went across the fields to the old cottage, with the crooked black timbers, and the odd bent chimney, from which came a curl of blue smoke.

'Who's living in the Crooked House?' wondered the little man, but he was too polite to ask. They went up the narrow flagged path, and flung open the door. A bright fire burned on the open hearth, and the three-legged table was set for tea, with a queer little blue teapot and the blue mug. There was a lop-sided loaf of bread, a pat of butter, and a honeycomb. In the middle of the table was a bunch of wild flowers, and between the fluttering blue curtains glowed the pot of geraniums.

'This is your house now,' said Mrs Dale, laughing at the little man's cries of astonishment and delight. 'You are to live here all your life. You can scare the crows, pick the herbs and flowers, cook your mushrooms, and do just as you like. You shall have new bread every baking-day, and as much curds and buttermilk as you want.'

She uncovered the baskets and took out pots of jam and some brown eggs. Then she led him up the winding stair to see his little bed with the dimity cover, and the bent chair by the side. He looked with admiration at the snowy walls, and the clean scrubbed floor with its rag-rug and sheepskin mat. The cat walked about, wrinkling her nose, and purring in content. Suddenly she made a dash and caught a mouse which had dared to peep at the newcomers.

'Look! It's a crooked mouse,' cried Mrs Dale, and indeed it was! On its back was a tiny hump, and the cat carried the little creature carefully to her master without hurting it, and laid it at his feet.

'It shall live alongside us,' said Crooked Tom, 'and then we shall all be crooked together!'

From that day they lived all three in the crooked little house – the crooked man, the crooked cat, and the crooked little mouse, and there was nobody happier than they were, for they had no cares, but took whatever came with simple joy.

In time to come a song was made about them, and it was sung all over the countryside. Here it is:

There was a crooked man, and he walked a crooked mile,
He found a crooked sixpence upon a crooked stile,
He bought a crooked cat, and it caught a crooked mouse,
And they all lived together in a crooked little house.

Guy Fawkes's Day

'Remember, remember the fifth of November,
Gunpowder, treason and plot.
I see no reason why gunpowder treason
Should ever be forgot.'

ANN PIG was singing the old rhyme as she scrubbed the table. Sam Pig was carrying water for her, and soaping the scrubbing-brush, but when he heard that song he stopped still.

'Sing that again, Sister Ann,' said he.

'Remember, remember the fifth of November,
Gunpowder, treason and plot,'

warbled Ann in her high squeaky little voice.

'What does it mean?' asked Sam. 'What is gunpowder-treason-and-plot?'

'I'm sure I don't know,' said Ann cheerfully. 'Give me the scrubbing-brush, Sam.'

'Something to eat maybe like macaroni-cheese or sardine-on-toast.' Sam dipped the brush in the water and handed it to his sister.

'Is it near the fifth of November now?'

'I don't know, Sam. You do ask some questions! The leaves have fallen, so it's nearly winter, but I don't know the date. Dates are no use to us. You must ask Brock. He'll know. He's got an almanac, with all the important days of the year in it.'

She went on scrubbing and singing her song. The table was white as a bone, but as the four pigs had no tablecloth there was a daily scrubbing.

'Where did you hear that song, Ann?' asked Sam.

'I think I heard a little boy down the lane sing it, or perhaps it was the ploughman, or the carter, or maybe the shepherd. Perhaps the robin sang it.'

'Or the fox,' said Sam. 'You don't seem to remember, although it's all about remembering.'

When Brock came home Sam ran to meet him. They walked up the garden path together, and Sam carried Brock's game-bag, and fishing-rod and stick.

'When is fifth of November?' asked Sam.

'Ah!' said Brock. 'Ah! After tea I will look in my almanac. We must be pretty near Guy Fawkes's Day. Pretty near Gunpowder, treason and plot day.'

'What does it mean. Brock? Ann was singing a song about it.'

'It's a Great Day, when children have fireworks and they eat treacle toffee and parkin, and they make bonfires and jump over them.'

'Oh Brock! Oh!' sighed Sam in rapture, but he didn't say any more.

When all the little pigs had finished tea, and washed up, Brock took out his pocket-book and looked at the almanac. He read out the chief days of the year and the little pigs listened to him.

'There's Swallow's Day, when the swallow comes back, and Cuckoo's Day when the cuckoo comes, and many a bird day, which changes a bit according to a secret which a few of us know. There's May Day, when the Maypole grows on the village greens. That's fixed. And there's Easter, when the stars dance, and Midsummer when the sun is the king. There's Hay-harvest when the hay is brought to the stacks, and Harvest Home, when the corn is gathered and stored. There's Saint Valentine's Day, when the birds get married, and Shooting Day when the pheasant is caught for the pot. I can't find any mention of Guy Fawkes's Day in my almanac.'

The little pigs were disappointed, and begged Brock to look again.

He turned over the queer brown pages of his book, and Sam got glimpses of strange pictures of birds and beasts and fishes, of sun and moon and stars.

'Here it is,' cried Brock at last. 'It's in small print. It isn't one of our own feast days, like May Day and Midwinter Day and Hibernating Day when I go to my castle for a rest. Here it is, a children's day. Oh goodness! It's quite soon. Tomorrow is Guy Fawkes's Day, the Fifth of November!'

'Oh Brock! What can we do? Can we eat that treason-and-plot?' they cried.

'That's a kind of treacle toffee. I think I could make it tonight if we have any treacle.'

'Yes. We've got a tin of treacle,' shouted Tom, leaping

up. 'It's in the store-cupboard. Little Sam brought it back from the Old Witch's house last year, when he stayed the night with her.'

'Of course,' cried Sam. 'She gave me a present of a treacle tin when I went to see her about a cuckoo-clock.'

Tom climbed on a chair to reach the top shelf of the cupboard. He lifted down the shiny tin and Ann dusted away the cobwebs and removed a few small animals which had taken up their winter quarters on the lid. They all dipped a spoon in it and had a taste. Yes, it was the delicious honey-sweet syrup Sam had brought home!

'Now for the treacle toffee,' cried Brock. 'A honeycomb, a tin of treacle, and a pound of butter all boiled together till the mixture sets when tested in a cup of cold water! That's treacle toffee.'

Bill brought out the saucepan and Sam licked it clean. Then Tom made up the fire with sticks from the woodshed, and Ann found the wooden spoon that Sam had carved for her Christmas present. All was ready and Brock took off his coat and slipped a white apron round him. He mixed the ingredients together, the honeycomb, the butter and the treacle, and stirred them over the fire. The honey melted, the butter melted, and the treacle melted, and they all joined together to make treacle toffee.

While the sticky mess bubbled and steamed and sent out its delicious smell, the four pigs danced round the room singing:

> '*Remember, remember the fifth of November,*
> *Gunpowder, treason and plot.*'

'The inside of a honey-bees' hive must smell like this,' said Ann Pig, sniffing the aroma.

'It's sweeter than a new haystack,' said Bill Pig.

'Or a bush of honeysuckle,' said Tom.

'Or a newly-ploughed field,' said Brock the Badger.

'What about the fireworks, Brock?' asked Sam. 'Tell us about them. Are they like our fire, burning bright on a frosty night?'

'Fireworks! Ah, Sam! Even on the frostiest night of shooting stars you've never seen the like of fireworks! It's like the Northern Lights in one's own garden! Sky rockets soar up to the heavens and burst in a shower of coloured stars. Catherine-wheels spin round like whirling suns with green-and-red rays. Golden fountains come showering out of little boxes. Roman candles burn with balloons of light. Jump-jacks make you leap as they dart after you.'

'Where have you seen them, Brock?' they asked.

'I've waited in dark lanes, outside gardens on Guy Fawkes's Day, and watched children play with them. I've been filled with wonder at them.'

'Where do they get them from, Brock? From the sky? From the fairies? From the little people themselves?'

'No. Fireworks belong to earth people. They are in shops, for sale like toys.'

'Oh, Brock. Could we? Could we? Do you think we could – ?'

'What? Buy fireworks?'

The pigs nodded.

Brock smoked his pipe for a few minutes in silence, and Sam stirred the treacle toffee for him. The rest stared at Brock and then sniffed at the toffee and then looked at Brock.

'Open the money-box,' said Brock at last.

Ann Pig took the holly-wood money-box from the mantelpiece and unlocked it. There was a little heap of precious pennies, all shiny and polished. Sam was the penny-polisher, and he always rubbed the coins with sand and wiped them clean when anybody found a penny.

'Will these buy fireworks?' the pigs asked anxiously.

'Yes. We can get quite a lot with those pence, for one of them is silver. I'll go to the village tomorrow and buy them.'

'Can I go with you, Badger?' asked Sam quickly.

'Certainly, Sam, if you're not afraid of being caught and carried off to a pig-sty,' laughed Brock.

'Of course not! Why, I'm quite well known nowadays, since I helped the farmer with his hay,' said Sam proudly.

The toffee was bubbling in the saucepan, and Brock showed the little pigs how to drop a spoonful into a cup of cold water to test it. There it lay like a little snake, curled round, hard and crisp. The toffee was done. Ann poured it into a wooden mould to set and when it was nearly cold she cut it into squares. There was a good pile of treacle toffee ready for Guy Fawkes's Day.

All the next morning the pigs gathered firewood ready for the bonfire. They piled it high like a stack. In the afternoon Brock and Sam Pig set out for the village. They walked along the fields and through the woods until they were near the outlying cottages. Then they took to the road, walking easily and quietly like two respectable little men, Brock with his hat pulled over his eyes and his pipe in his mouth, Sam with his haymaking hat over his ears, and his plaid trousers and Sunday coat. Brock puffed and puffed at his baccy and Sam carried a bag to hold the fire-works. The little pig was so excited that he kept starting to run, but Badger shook his head and warned him to be careful.

'Don't 'ee run unless you're forced,' said he.

They passed the barber's shop with the pole painted in red and white stripes, and they peeped inside at a man having a shave. They crossed the market-place by the Blue Boar Inn and saw old men drinking their ale by the fire.

'That blue pig is a relation of yours,' whispered Brock, and Sam nodded and looked up at the picture of the great tusked boar which hung above his head.

Then they came to the fireworks shop. It was usually a a sweetshop, where old Mrs Bunting sold humbugs and pear-drops, but the little bow-fronted window was now full of bright red fireworks. Brock and Sam pressed their noses to the pane and whispered together about them, and talked of those they would buy.

'I'll go in alone,' said Brock. 'I can explain to Mrs Bunting more easily by myself. You wait for me, and don't go away or you'll get lost. Don't speak to anybody, and don't do anything you didn't ought.'

'No. I won't do nuffin,' said Sam.

Brock hitched up his trousers, settled his hat, and entered the shop. The bell jangled, and old Mrs Bunting came from her kitchen to serve him. Little Sam could see them talking and examining the red packets which held all the mysteries of coloured fire. He waited by the window, staring at the fireworks, peering at the jar of sweets on the shelf, and wondering about the strange pink masks of faces with holes for eyes and cardboard noses which lay among the fireworks.

Brock was a long time, and Sam got tired of waiting. His legs ached with the long walk, his coat was uncomfortable. He looked about him for somewhere to sit down, and there, just round the corner, was a crooked old chair, with a couple of poles through it. It might have been made for Sam!

'Just what I want! How kind of somebody,' thought Sam, and he sat down and leaned his head against the broken chair-back. In less than a minute he had fallen asleep.

'Look here!' cried a little boy. 'Here's somebody's guy! Somebody's left his guy here. Let's go off with it. It's a fine one with a pig's face.'

'It's Tommy Bunting's guy. He's gone home for tea. He told us he was going to make a good guy from a pillow and some old clothes and a mask from his grannie's shop. Let's go off and get some money with it before he comes back,' said another boy.

'Oh, what a lark!' cried the first boy.

They seized the poles and carried off the chair with Sam Pig fast asleep. When Brock came out of the shop there was no Sam.

'The rascal! He's got tired of waiting and gone home without me,' grumbled Brock. 'Still, I don't often get the chance of talking to a sensible old woman who remembers days of long ago.'

Brock glanced round and then padded off with his bag of fireworks through the village towards home.

Sam slept soundly in the comfortable old chair, rocked by the swaying motion.

'Penny for the guy,' chanted the boys and pence came rattling into the tin mug they held out, for never was seen such a queer little, odd little guy as the one that sat in the high-backed chair.

'It's a heavy old guy! It must have got some good stuffing to make it like this,' groaned the boys, and they plodded along the village street from door to door, tapping and showing their guy.

After an unusually hard bump Sam Pig awoke. He looked around with wonderment, and he listened to the boys' song:

'Remember, remember the fifth of November,
Gunpowder, treason and plot.
There is no reason why gunpowder treason
Should ever be forgot.'

'A penny for the guy, please. Thank you, sir. A penny for the guy.'

They rattled their tin mug and collected the pence and Sam Pig sat in the chair, very much surprised. He was quite cheerful, and he enjoyed himself after the first moment of fright when he found himself swaying about between two little boys. He looked around him, at the cottages, at the children counting their fireworks, at the farm labourers riding back to tea on the cart-horses, at the women setting their tables in the jolly kitchens, at the open doors where firelight shone on chests of drawers and china dogs and sanded stone floors.

'Here am I, little Sam Pig, going for a ride with two boys as horses,' he told himself, and he smiled with happiness.

'That's a fine guy you've got there,' said Old Gaffer Snow. 'Minds me of a porker more'n anything.'

He put his wrinkled hand deep in his trouser pocket and brought out a halfpenny.

'A halfpenny for your guy,' said he.

'Thank you, Gaffer,' said the boys.

'What are ye going to do wi' him?' asked the old man.

'We've got a grand bonfire on the green, and we're going to put him on it when it's dark enough,' said they.

Sam Pig started! Had he heard aright? Put him on a bonfire? Roast him?

'He'll make a grand big blaze, will that guy,' said Old Gaffer. 'Where did ye get him?'

'We found him outside Mother Bunting's shop. I think he belongs to Tom.'

'What's he made of?' asked the Gaffer, stepping forward. 'He looks kind of natural to me.'

'I don't know. Stuffing or rags or something,' said the boys. But the Gaffer stretched out a finger and thumb and gave Sam's leg a pinch.

'Oh! O-o-o-oh!' squealed Sam, and he struggled to his feet and started to run.

'Hey! He's alive! After him! Catch him! He's running away. He's a somebody, not a guy at all,' shouted the boys and they scampered after Sam.

'I didna think he was a guy,' chuckled the old Gaffer. 'My eyes don't deceive me, although I'm well on ninety years. I thought he was a porker and a porker he is.'

But Sam Pig was legging it down the village, and over the stream, and across the market-place. The ostler came out from the Blue Boar and shouted, 'Whoa, there!' but Sam hurried on. The barber ran out from his shop and waved his towel at Sam, but Sam ran the faster. He left all behind him and trotted through the woods, and over the fields and under the hedges, till he arrived panting at the little house.

It was nearly dark when he got there, and Brock was standing at the door looking out for him.

'Hallo, Sam! You're late. You seem to be in a hurry. Anything the matter? Where have you been?'

'Oh! my goodness,' panted Sam. 'I've been a guy. I know all about Guy Fawkes now. He goes for a ride up and down the street and then, oh! Badger, they put him on a bonfire! But they didn't catch me! I was too quick for them!'

'Sam! A guy! Oh, Sam, and you in your best Sunday coat, and wearing your check trousers and your hay-making hat! Did they call you a guy?' Ann was indignant at the insult to her brother.

But Tom and Bill laughed uproariously, and nodded their heads and rolled on the floor in delight.

'Guy Pig! Little Guy Pig! That's your name! Oh, Sam, why didn't you stay a little longer and see the bonfire?'

'That's enough,' said Brock sternly. 'No more teasing. Sam might have had his curly tail singed. Now come along and stand in a row and hold out your hands. I've divided the fireworks into four parts, and each of you will have your own share to let off. It's dark enough now, and we will all go outside.'

Brock filled their hands with fireworks, a big catherine-wheel and a little one each, a couple of rockets, and many a fine firework. Ann divided the treacle toffee and out they went.

First of all they lighted the bonfire, and watched the flames shoot up like feathers, and the sticks crackle and blaze.

Then came the fireworks. The catherine-wheels spun with green and red spikes of flame, when Brock pinned them to an oak tree. The jump-jacks leaped about in the wood like live creatures, and the little pigs ran away from them, shrieking with laughter. The rockets soared high above the tree-tops nearly to the stars, and then burst into coloured lights.

'Oh-oh-oh-oh!' called the little pigs, opening wide their round eyes as they watched them.

The golden fountains and Roman candles sent out their curving waterfalls of bright fire. There were bangs and cracks and sparkles, and every animal in the wood peered anxiously from behind trees to find out what was the matter.

'It's those pigs playing with fire and gunpowder! I wonder Brock the Badger allows it! Such goings-on!' they said crossly, and they retired to their deepest holes and shelters.

The four pigs and Brock were dancing among the sparkles and prickles of flame, and their voices came clear in the November air.

'Remember, remember the fifth of November,
Gunpowder, treason and plot.'

They leapt over the dying flames of the bonfire, and roasted potatoes in the ashes. They ate their toffee and shouted and laughed with glee. Then the last firework fizzled out, and the last rocket soared to the sky. The last cracker banged and the last piece of treacle toffee was eaten. Away they went to bed, and once more the woods were silent and the stars looked down at the great old trees.

The Singing Gate

SAM PIG went out to swing on the big gate one fine morning. This was no ordinary gate to a garden or field path, or even to a ploughfield with a scarecrow in the middle. It was a five-barred gate of oak, which shut in Farmer Greensleeves' best field of meadow grass for hay-making. It was the gate where Sally the Mare often lingered to gaze at the hills and the sky and the tree-tops. It was the gate which shut with such a resounding clang that the echo of it rang through the countryside, to tell all people that Farmer Greensleeves' best meadow was not to be entered until the grass had grown long, and the hay-makers and mowers had arrived for the hay-harvest.

Sam liked this gate for many reasons. It was his own meeting place with Sally the Mare. He could count on her being there most evenings when she wasn't in the stable. It was the gate Sam climbed when he wanted to mount on Sally's back. Best of all, it was a singing gate.

Sam swung backwards and forwards on it, when it wasn't shut to keep the mowing grass safe, and the gate sang with a shrill cry, going up and down the scale with the motion. Sam loved this gate-music. He, too, sang when the gate sang and together they made a loud squealing noise like a dozen pigs squeezed in a farm cart together.

'Sam Pig, Sam Pig, every afternoon,
Come and sit along o' me, and sing a little tune,'

went the gate, in its cheerful inviting voice.

Little Sam Pig listened to it, with his head aside and his ears cocked. Then he replied in his own sing-song:

'Oak gate, meadow gate,
I'll sit along o' you.
I'm weary of my family,
I wants to be with you.'

Then, after some more swinging and singing, the gate would shut itself fast to the gate-post, and Sam knew that the song was finished. It was time for something else to happen.

'Let's have a tale now,' Sam would say, and the gate rumbled and mumbled, and shook its wooden gate-post, and rattled its iron latch as it thought deep in its oaken heart. Then, with little soft murmurs like the droppings of shavings from a carpenter's plane, the gate began to talk.

'Once upon a time I was a young oak tree in yonder wood,' it began, and Sam's blue eyes opened wide. Over the field was a wood where the pheasants lived, and the trees grew close together making a deep black shade. It was a wood on a hillside, with rocks sticking out like dragons, and, indeed, one of these rocks was a real dragon, which had fallen asleep a thousand years ago. It was a wood with many wild flowers in the glades, and a game-keeper's tree, where robber birds hung. Sam never ventured in this wood, for he was afraid of the game-keeper. He always ran on the tiny footpath which skirted the trees, but occasionally he poked his nose over the wall, or he hunted for bilberries on the bushes at the wood's edge. In this enchanted wood, with its dragon, its giants, and fairies, the oak tree had been born.

'When I was a young oak tree, I sheltered a man running away from those who were after him. He climbed my boughs, and I spread my leaves over his face to hide him,' said the gate.

'Who was after him?' asked Sam. 'A bear?'

'No, some men dressed in armour: soldiers they were. He was a King Charles man, so I heard afterwards. I hid him and kept him safe, and a friend at the farm brought him food and looked after him, until he could escape.'

'Did he say Thank you?' asked Sam.

'Yes, Sam, he did. Years afterwards he returned and found me and cut a little cross of thankfulness on my trunk.'

'I should like to save somebody,' said Sam, slowly stroking the gate.

'You never know,' said the gate. 'Now you tell me a tale, Sam. It's your turn.'

Sam began the tale of the circus, with its wonders, and he was in the middle of it, with the oak gate listening with all its ears, when Sally came up.

'Farmer Greensleeves is bringing the young bull to

this meadow,' said Sally. 'You'd best get out of the way, Sam.'

'Why?' asked Sam. 'I like bulls. They roar and stamp.'

'You won't like this one,' said Sally sharply. 'So move away. He's a fierce fellow, bad-tempered too. He won't be here very long, it's my opinion.'

The Farmer and his man came across the field with a young bull with a ring in his nose, and a pole holding him from them. Sam scuttled away and watched from the shelter of the hedge. Sally strolled off and began to eat the grass. The man opened the gate and the bull was turned into the field.

'I'll lock this gate, for it's a danger place,' said Farmer Greensleeves. 'Nobody must come in with that young demon. They won't want to stop very long if they do get in.'

The bull galloped off with his tail uplifted like a question mark. Farmer Greensleeves took a padlock from his pocket and locked the gate. Then he caught sight of Sam squinting from the hedge.

'No more swinging on the gate for a while, Sam,' said he. 'Not while the bull is here. Gate's got to be kept shut.'

Sam nodded. 'No, Master. I'll sit on the gate but I won't unfasten it,' said he. 'I can listen to the tales just the same.'

The Farmer put up a notice, 'Beware of the Bull', and went away. Sam and Sally came close to look at it.

'What does it say?' asked Sally. 'You can read it, can't you, Sam?'

Sam slowly spelled the words.

'Bee and Bull,' said he. 'B is for Brock the Badger.

Something to do with Brock and Bees and Bull,' he informed Sally.

''Ware Bull,' said the gate. 'I've had this before.'

Sam climbed up and sat on the top bar to get a good look at the young bull.

'What's the matter, Bull?' called Sam, as the bull rushed up and down, but the beast only roared angrily. Then it began to eat the good sweet grass and Sam forgot all about it.

'This gate and me is telling tales,' said Sam to Sally. 'We are good friends, we are.'

'This gate is a special one,' agreed Sally. 'The children at the farm call it the Wishing Gate. They come here and make their wishes.'

'Do the wishes come true?' asked Sam.

'I can't tell you for certain. It depends what you mean by true. I only know what I've heard. Often and often, young Dick has ridden on my back to this gate and here he has stopped and put a hand on the top bar where you're sitting and made a wish.'

'What did he wish for?' asked Sam. 'Surely he has everything in the world – a farm and you, and lots to eat!'

'He wished not to have to go to school, and not to have to go to bed, and then he wanted to see the circus, and he asked for a football,' said Sally.

'What then?' demanded Sam.

'Well, he fell off the haystack and hurt his leg, so he didn't have to go to school. He got that wish. He stayed up late and he was so tired he begged to go to bed, so he got that wish. He went to the circus, and he had a football, so his wishes came true,' said Sally.

'Can I make a wish?' asked Sam.

'Of course you can, Sam. You've made many a wish, on stars and moons, and now make one at our old Wishing Gate.'

'I wish . . . I wish . . .' began Sam, and then there was a shout. A man was running in the field and the bull was after him.

'He shouldn't have come,' said Sam. 'He was picking our mushrooms. He must have climbed the far wall. If he'd come this way he would have seen the notice.'

Sally watched the man with anxiety. The bull was getting nearer, and the man ran this way and that in terror. The heavy strong animal kept its head lowered, and its sharp wicked horns were ready to toss the man. He tried to climb the wall, but there was no foothold and he ran desperately towards the gate across the wide field.

'Poor fellow,' said Sally. 'He can't run fast enough. He's too fat. He'll be caught.'

Sam made up his mind. He put his short little legs over the top bar and slid to the ground. Then he ran towards the bull, shouting and waving his hat. The bull's attention was diverted for a moment.

'What's this?' he roared, turning his great head to Sam, and his blood-shot eyes glared. 'Who's this impudent creature?'

He made a rush at Sam, and the man sprinted to the gate and got over in a flash. There stood Sally the Mare with her nose raised, as she whinnied to encourage Sam.

'Run! Sam, run!' she called, in her own language, and the man stared at Sally and then watched the race in the field. Sam dodged one way and the bull dodged the same.

Then Sam made a dive under the bull's nose and came out behind his legs. That gave him a chance, and as the bull looked down to find him, Sam flew with all four legs twinkling, and little tail outstretched and little mouth calling: 'Wee, wee, wee,' just like an ordinary little pig in a farmyard.

'Come on, Sam,' called Sally, and the man at the gate clapped his hands and shouted, 'Run, little 'un. Run.'

Sam scuttled to the gate and scrambled over just in time, for the bull arrived as Sam dropped safely to the other side.

'Well run, Sam,' said Sally, licking him with her soft tongue.

'It's a pig,' muttered the man. 'One of Farmer Greensleeves' pets. Well, he's saved my bacon!'

Then he looked up and saw the notice, 'Beware of the Bull'.

'A bit late,' said he, 'but better late than never.'

Sam looked at him and he looked at Sam. 'They'll not believe it when I tell 'em at the Pig and Whistle tonight,' said he. 'But it's true, isn't it, young pig? You did save me, didn't you?'

Sam nodded, with never a word. Then the little pig picked up a dandelion and stuck it in his mouth.

'It's true. I'm not dreaming,' said the man, walking away. 'There's the bull and there's the pig and here am I, Samuel Ramsbottom. But they won't believe it, down at the Pig and Whistle.'

'He never said "Thank you",' murmured Sam sadly. He climbed on the gate and watched the bull. In the distance lay a red spotted handkerchief full of mushrooms the man had dropped in his flight.

'I think I'll get those for Tom to cook for supper,' said Sam.

'Best wait a bit,' advised Sally. 'Wait till the bull lies down and takes a nap. He won't be long. He's upset and cross. Don't bother him now.'

So Sam sat on the gate waiting, and as he sat he sang another song to the old gate:

'*Sam Pig, Ann Pig, Tom, Bill and Brock,*
Went swinging on the old gate to taste the lock.
The gate was made of oakenwood, the lock was made of money,
The latch was sugar candy and the gate-posts sweetest honey.'

'That's a queer 'un,' said Sally, as she listened to Sam.

'It's my imagination,' said Sam airily. 'You never know what might happen.'

'No, you're right about that,' agreed Sally.

'I'm hungry after that run,' said Sam. 'I could eat some sugar candy and honey now this minute.'

He leaned close to the latch and put out his little pink tongue. He took a lick and another lick. It was sweet as sugar candy. Then he licked the gate-post. It was sweet as honey. A bee rose from it, and left a morsel there it had just taken from the cloverpatch.

'Sally. Sally. My wish has come true,' cried Sam, and he licked again.

Sally stared at Sam and then she too came to the gate. She rubbed her nose on it. Indeed the latch was sweet tasting.

'You've done it, Sam. I feel sugar on my lips, and there's a taste of honey round the gate-posts.'

They both were silent while they licked, and suddenly Sam laughed.

'There's nothing. It was my imagination, Sally.'

'A powerful imagination to make sugar candy and honey out of an old gate,' said Sally. 'But there's the bull gone to sleep, and you've got a chance.'

Sam ran off, dancing softly, past the snoring bull to the far part of the field and he returned with the red handkerchief full of mushrooms.

'I wanted a new hanky,' said he. 'This is my reward.' He ate a few fresh button mushrooms and then strolled away with Sally. They both walked to the barn and there they nibbled brown linseed cake, put ready for the cows.

'I like cow-cake,' said Sam Pig.

It was good solid food and they felt better for it. Sam filled his pocket with the cake, and then he made a little whistle-pipe from an oaten straw.

'You go home now,' said Sally. 'I've to do some work for Master, and you go home.'

Sam said good night, but he went round by the singing gate for a last word and a look at the bull. The fierce animal was quietly grazing and, when Sam played a tune on his whistle-pipe, it came to the gate.

'Sorry I was so fierce today, Sam,' it said, apologetically. 'That man roused me, and I was hot and tired and thirsty. I feel better now.'

'It's all right,' said Sam, amiably offering the cow-cake to the bull. 'I quite understand. I feel that way myself often when Tom has been teasing me.'

The bull settled down on one side of the gate, and Sam stretched out his hand and stroked the bull's nose. A little song came out of the air, and perhaps it was the gate singing, for it cannot have been the bull. This is what Sam heard:

'Over the hills to China
Over the mountains to Spain.
Carry him off to dreamland,
And bring him back again.'

The gate gently rocked Sam, till he fell asleep. He rolled down and lay curled up by the bull. There Farmer Greensleeves found him when he went at dusk to look at his animal.

'Sam Pig. What are you doing here?' he cried, and he lifted Sam up by his trousers and set him at the right side of the gate.

Sam rubbed his eyes and yawned. Then he picked up his whistle-pipe and looked at the sleeping bull.

'Oh, Master. I've been taming the bull,' said he. 'Then the gate sang a song to me and I fell asleep.'

'I'm not surprised at anything you do or anything the old gate does,' said the Farmer. 'Now you go home quick before anything catches you. Where did you get that red handkerchief?'

'It was a mushroomer's hanky, and the bull made him run,' said Sam, and both he and the Farmer laughed.

The Farmer put a hand in one of his big pockets and brought out a rosy apple. He put his hand in another pocket and brought out a juicy pear. He felt in his left-hand trouser pocket and found a few humbugs. He felt in his right-hand pocket and found a piece of sugar candy.

'Here, take these, Sam. They'll do for your supper,' said he. 'I always keep a few bits in my pockets to eat when I'm peckish.'

'Oh, thank you, Master,' said Sam joyfully. 'I wish I had all those pockets. I would fill them with food for a week.'

He ran off, hurrying home to Brock the Badger, who was standing by the door looking up at the moon, and counting the early stars.

'Brock,' he cried. 'I've been to sleep. I needn't go to bed. I've had a dream, Brock.'

'What did you dream?' asked Brock.

'I dreamt I went to China and to Spain,' said Sam.

'What were they like, Sam?' asked little Ann, running up when she heard her young brother's voice.

'China was full of dragons, and Spain was full of cats,' said Sam. 'I was just inviting them to come home with me when Farmer Greensleeves woke me up.'

'Come indoors and sit by the fire,' invited Brock. 'I'll tell you a tale about a badger who went to China and brought a blue dragon home with him.'

So they sat with Brock and listened to his story, while the clock ticked, and the fire crackled, and the kettle sang on the hearth.

'I'm glad we live here,' said Ann, cosily. 'I like a little house all by itself, and nobody can find it, because Brock has magicked it. Then no dragons and cats can come.'

'I saved a man today,' said Sam, suddenly. 'I saved him and he gave me his handkerchief for a reward. At least, I took it.'

'Did you save him from a dragon?' asked Tom Pig.

'No, from a raging bull,' replied Sam casually. 'I was a bull-fighter.'

'Then you really went to Spain, Sam,' said Brock. 'That's where the bull-fighters live.'

'I suppose I did,' said Sam. 'Yes, I fought the bull and then I fed him on cow-cake. Yes. That's all.'

Christmas is Coming

AT Christmas the wind ceased to moan. Snow lay thick on the fields and the woods cast blue shadows across it. The fir trees were like sparkling, gem-laden Christmas trees, the only ones Susan had ever seen. The orchard, with the lacy old boughs outlined with snow, was a grove of fairy trees. The woods were enchanted, exquisite, the trees were holy, and anything harmful had shrunken to a thin wisp and had retreated into the depths.

The fields lay with their unevennesses gone and paths obliterated, smooth white slopes criss-crossed by black lines running up to the woods. More than ever the farm seemed under a spell, like a toy in the forest, with little wooden animals and men; a brown horse led by a stiff little red-scarfed man to a yellow stable door; round, white, woolly sheep clustering round a blue trough of orange mangolds; red cows drinking from a square white trough, and returning to a painted cow-house.

Footprints were everywhere on the snow, rabbits and foxes, blackbirds, pheasants and partridges, trails of small paws, the mark of a brush, and the long feet of the cock pheasant and the tip-mark of his tail.

A jay flew out of the wood like a blue flashing diamond and came to the grass-plot for bread. A robin entered the house and hopped under the table while Susan sat very still and her father sprinkled crumbs on the floor.

Rats crouched outside the window, peeping out of the walls with gleaming eyes, seizing the birds' crumbs and scraps, and slowly lolloping back again.

Red squirrels ran along the walls to the back door, close to the window, to eat the crumbs on the bench where the milk-cans froze. Every wild animal felt that a truce had come with the snow, and they visited the house where there was food in plenty, and sat with paws uplifted and noses twitching.

For the granaries were full, it had been a prosperous year, and there was food for everyone. Not like the year before when there was so little hay that Mr Garland had to buy a stack in February. Three large haystacks as big as houses stood in the stackyard, thatched evenly and straight by Job Fletcher, who was the best thatcher for many a mile. Great mounds showed where the roots were buried. The brick-lined pit was filled with grains and in the barns were stores of corn.

The old brew-house was full of logs of wood, piled high against the walls, cut from trees which the wind had blown down. The coal-house with its strong ivied walls, part of the old fortress, had been stored with coal brought many a mile in the blaze of summer; twenty tons lay under the snow.

On the kitchen walls hung the sides of bacon and from hooks in the ceiling dangled great hams and shoulders. Bunches of onions were twisted in the pantry and barn, and an empty cow-house was stored with potatoes for immediate use.

The floor of the apple chamber was covered with apples, rosy apples, little yellow ones, like cowslip balls, wizenedy apples with withered, wrinkled cheeks, fat, well-fed, smooth-faced apples, and immense green cookers, pointed like a house, which would burst in the oven and pour out a thick cream of the very essence of apples.

Even the cheese chamber had its cheeses this year, for there had been too much milk for the milkman, and the cheese presses had been put into use again. Some of them were Christmas cheese, with layers of sage running through the middles like green ribbons.

Stone jars like those in which the forty thieves hid stood on the pantry floor, filled with white lard, and balls of fat tied up in bladders hung from the hooks. Along the broad shelves round the walls were pots of jam, blackberry and apple, from the woods and orchard, Victoria plum from the trees on house and barn, black currant from the garden, and red currant jelly, damson cheese from the half-wild ancient trees which grew everywhere, leaning over walls, dropping their blue fruit on paths and walls, in pig-sty and orchard, in field and water-trough, so that Susan thought they were wild as hips and haws.

Pickles and spices filled old brown pots decorated with crosses and flowers, like the pitchers and crocks of Will Shakespeare's time.

In the little dark wine chamber under the stairs were

bottles of elderberry wine, purple, thick, and sweet, and golden cowslip wine, and hot ginger, some of them many years old, waiting for the winter festivities.

There were dishes piled with mince pies on the shelves of the larder, and a row of plum puddings with their white calico caps, and strings of sausages, and round pats of butter, with swans and cows and wheat-ears printed upon them.

Everyone who called at the farm had to eat and drink at Christmas-tide.

A few days before Christmas Mr Garland and Dan took a bill-hook and knife and went into the woods to cut branches of scarlet-berried holly. They tied them together with ropes and dragged them down over the fields to the barn. Mr Garland cut a bough of mistletoe from the ancient hollow hawthorn which leaned over the wall by the orchard, and thick clumps of dark-berried ivy from the walls.

Indoors, Mrs Garland and Susan and Becky polished and rubbed and cleaned the furniture and brasses, so that everything glowed and glittered. They decorated every room, from the kitchen where every lustre jug had its sprig in its mouth, every brass candlestick had its chaplet, every copper saucepan and preserving-pan had its wreath of shining berries and leaves, through the hall, which was a bower of green, to the two parlours which were festooned and hung with holly and boughs of fir, and ivy berries dipped in red raddle, left over from sheep marking.

Holly decked every picture and ornament. Sprays hung over the bacon and twisted round the hams and herb bunches. The clock carried a crown on his head, and every dish-cover had a little sprig. Susan kept an eye on the lonely forgotten humble things, the jelly moulds and colanders and nutmeg-graters, and made them happy with glossy leaves. Everything seemed to speak, to ask for its morsel of greenery, and she tried to leave out nothing.

On Christmas Eve fires blazed in the kitchen and parlour and even in the bedrooms. Becky ran from room to room with the red-hot salamander which she stuck between the bars to make a blaze, and Mrs Garland took the copper warming-pan filled with glowing cinders from the kitchen fire and rubbed it between the sheets of all the beds. Susan had come down to her cosy tiny room with thick curtains at the window, and a fire in the big fire-place. Flames roared up the chimneys as Dan carried in the logs and Becky piled them on the blaze. The wind came back and tried to get in, howling at the keyholes, but all the shutters were cottered and the doors shut. The horses and mares stood in the stables, warm and happy, with nodding heads. The cows slept in the cow-houses, the sheep in the open sheds. Only Rover stood at the door of his kennel, staring up at the sky, howling to the dog in the moon, and then he, too, turned and lay down in his straw.

In the middle of the kitchen ceiling there hung the kissing-bunch, the best and brightest pieces of holly made in the shape of a large ball which dangled from the hook. Silver and gilt drops, crimson bells, blue glass trumpets, bright oranges and red polished apples, peeped and glittered through the glossy leaves. Little flags of all nations, but chiefly Turkish for some unknown reason, stuck out like quills on a hedgehog. The lamp hung near, and every little berry, every leaf, every pretty ball and apple had a tiny yellow flame reflected in its heart.

Twisted candles hung down, yellow, red, and blue, unlighted but gay, and on either side was a string of paper lanterns.

Mrs Garland climbed on a stool and nailed on the wall the Christmas texts, 'God bless our Home', 'God is Love', 'Peace be on this House', 'A Happy Christmas and a Bright New Year'.

So the preparations were made. Susan hung up her stocking at the foot of the bed and fell asleep. But soon singing roused her and she sat, bewildered. Yes, it was the carol-singers.

Outside under the stars she could see the group of men and women, with lanterns throwing beams across the paths and on to the stable door. One man stood apart beating time, another played a fiddle and another had a flute. The rest sang in four parts the Christmas hymns, 'While shepherds watched', 'O come, all ye faithful', and 'Hark the herald angels sing'.

There was the Star, Susan could see it twinkling and bright in the dark boughs with their white frosted layers; and there was the stable. In a few hours it would be Christmas Day, the best day of all the year.

The Riddle-me-Ree

'In marble walls as white as milk,
Lined with a skin as soft as silk,
Within a fountain crystal clear,
A golden apple doth appear.
No doors there are to this strong-hold
Yet thieves break in and steal the gold.'

LITTLE TIM RABBIT asked this riddle when he came home from school one day.

Mrs Rabbit stood with her paws on her hips, admiring her young son's cleverness.

'It's a fine piece of poetry,' said she.

'It's a riddle,' said Tim. 'It's a riddle-me-ree. Do you know the answer, Mother?'

'No, Tim.' Mrs Rabbit shook her head. 'I'm not good at riddles. We'll ask your Father when he comes home. I can hear him stamping his foot outside. He knows everything, does Father.'

Mr Rabbit came bustling in. He flung down his bag of green food, mopped his forehead, and gave a deep sigh.

'There! I've collected enough for a family of elephants. I got lettuces, carrots, wild thyme, primrose leaves and tender shoots. I hope you'll make a good salad, Mother.'

'Can you guess a riddle?' asked Tim.

'I hope so, my son. I used to be very good at riddles. What is a Welsh Rabbit? Cheese! Ha ha!'

'Say it again, Tim,' urged Mrs Rabbit. 'It's such a good piece of poetry, and all.'

So Tim Rabbit stood up, put his hands behind his back, tilted his little nose and stared at the ceiling. Then in a high squeak he recited his new riddle:

'In marble walls as white as milk,
Lined with a skin as soft as silk,
Within a fountain crystal clear,
A golden apple doth appear.
No doors there are to this strong-hold,
Yet thieves break in and steal the gold.'

Father Rabbit scratched his head, and frowned.

'Marble walls,' said he. 'Hum! Ha! That's a palace. A golden apple. No doors. I can't guess it. Who asked it, Tim?'

'Old Jonathan asked us at school today. He said anyone who could guess it should have a prize. We can hunt and we can holler, we can ask and beg, but we must give him the answer by tomorrow.'

'I'll have a good think, my son,' said Mr Rabbit. 'We mustn't be beaten by a riddle.'

All over the common Father Rabbits were saying, 'I'll have a good think,' but not one Father knew the answer, and all the small bunnies were trying to guess.

Tim Rabbit met Old Man Hedgehog down the lane. The old fellow was carrying a basket of crab-apples for his youngest daughter. On his head he wore a round hat made from a cabbage leaf. Old Man Hedgehog was rather deaf, and Tim had to shout.

'Old Man Hedgehog. Can you guess a riddle?' shouted Tim.

'Eh?' The Hedgehog put his hand up to his ear. 'Eh?'

'A riddle!' cried Tim.

'Aye. I knows a riddle,' said Old Hedgehog. He put down his basket and lighted his pipe. 'Why does a Hedgehog cross a road? Eh? Why, for to get to t'other side.' Old Hedgehog laughed wheezily.

'Do you know this one?' shouted Tim.

'Which one? Eh?'

'In marble walls as white as milk,' said Tim loudly.

'I could do with a drop of milk,' said Hedgehog.

'Lined with a skin as soft as silk,' shouted Tim.

'Nay, my skin isn't like silk. It's prickly, is a Hedgehog's skin,' said the Old Hedgehog.

'Within a fountain crystal clear,' yelled Tim.

'Yes. I knows it. Down the field. There's a spring of water, clear as crystal. Yes, that's it,' cried Old Hedgehog, leaping about in excitement. 'That's the answer, a spring.'

'A golden apple doth appear,' said Tim, doggedly.

'A gowd apple? Where? Where?' asked Old Hedgehog, grabbing Tim's arm.

'No doors there are to this strong-hold,' said Tim, and now his voice was getting hoarse.

'No doors? How do you get in?' cried the Hedgehog.

'Yet thieves break in and steal the gold.' Tim's throat was sore with shouting. He panted with relief.

'Thieves? That's the Fox again. Yes. That's the answer.'

'No. It isn't the answer,' said Tim patiently.

'I can't guess a riddle like that. Too long. No sense in it,' said Old Man Hedgehog at last. 'I can't guess 'un. Now here's a riddle for you. It's my own, as one might say. My own!'

'What riddle is that?' asked Tim.

'Needles and Pins, Needles and Pins,
When Hedgehog marries his trouble begins.'

'What's the answer? I give it up,' said Tim.

'Why, Hedgehog. Needles and Pins, that's me.' Old Man Hedgehog threw back his head and stamped his feet and roared with laughter, and little Tim laughed too. They laughed and they laughed.

'Needles and Pins. Darning needles and hair pins,' said Old Hedgehog.

There was a rustle behind them, and they both sprang round, for Old Hedgehog could smell even if he was hard of hearing.

Out of the bushes poked a sharp nose, and a pair of bright eyes glinted through the leaves. A queer musky smell filled the air.

'I'll be moving on,' said Old Man Hedgehog. 'You'd best be getting along home too, Tim Rabbit. Your Mother wants you. Good day. Good day.'

Old Hedgehog trotted away, but the Fox stepped out and spoke in a polite kind of way.

'Excuse me,' said he. 'I heard merry laughter and I'm feeling rather blue. I should like a good laugh. What's the joke?'

'Old Man Hedgehog said he was needles and pins,' stammered poor little Tim Rabbit, edging away.

'Yes. Darning needles and hair pins,' said the Fox. 'Why?'

'It was a riddle,' said Tim.

'What about riddles?' asked the Fox.

> '*Marble milk, skin silk.*
> *Fountain clear, apple appear.*
> *No doors. Thieves gold,*'

Tim gabbled.

'Nonsense. Rubbish,' said the Fox. 'It isn't sense. I know a much better riddle.'

'What is it, sir?' asked Tim, forgetting his fright.

'Who is the fine gentleman in the red jacket who leads the hunt?' asked the Fox, with his head aside.

'I can't guess at all,' said Tim.

'A Fox. A Fox of course. He's the finest gentleman at the hunt.' He laughed so much at his own riddle that little Tim Rabbit had time to escape down the lane and to get home to his mother.

'Well, has anyone guessed the riddle?' asked Mrs Rabbit.

'Not yet, Mother, but I'm getting on,' said Tim.

Out he went again in the opposite direction, and he met the Mole.

'Can you guess a riddle, Mole?' he asked.

'Of course I can,' answered the Mole. Here it is:

'A little black man in a hole,
Pray tell me if he is a Mole,
If he's dressed in black velvet,
He's Moldy Warp Delvet,
He's a Mole, up a pole, in a hole.'

'I didn't mean that riddle,' said Tim.

'I haven't time for anybody else's riddles,' said the Mole, and in a flurry of soil he disappeared into the earth.

'He never stopped to listen to my recitation,' said Tim sadly.

He ran on, over the fields. There were Butterflies to hear his riddle, and Bumble-bees and Frogs, but they didn't know the answer. They all had funny little riddles of their own and nobody could help Tim Rabbit. So on he went across the wheatfield, right up to the farmyard, and he put his nose under the gate. That was as far as he dare go.

'Hallo, Tim Rabbit,' said the Cock. 'What do you want today?'

'Pray tell me the answer to a riddle,' said Tim politely. 'I've brought a pocketful of corn for a present. I gathered it in the cornfield on the way.'

The Cock called the Hens to listen to Tim's riddle. They came in a crowd, clustering round the gate, chattering loudly. Tim Rabbit settled himself on a stone so that they could see him. He wasn't very big, and there were many of them, clucking and whispering and shuffling their feet and shaking their feathers.

'Silence!' cried the Cock. 'Silence for Tim Rabbit.'

The Hens stopped shuffling and lifted their heads to listen.

Once more Tim recited his poem, and once more here it is:

> *'In marble walls as white as milk,*
> *Lined with a skin as soft as silk,*
> *Within a fountain crystal clear,*
> *A golden apple doth appear.*
> *No doors there are to this strong-hold,*
> *Yet thieves break in and steal the gold.'*

There was silence for a moment as Tim finished, and then such a rustle and murmur and tittering began, and the Hens put their little beaks together, and chortled and fluttered their wings and laughed in their sleeves.

'We know! We know!' they clucked.

'What is it?' asked Tim.

'An egg,' they all shouted together, and their voices were so shrill the farmer's wife came to the door to see what was the matter.

So Tim threw the corn among them, and thanked them for their cleverness.

'And here's a white egg to take home with you, Tim,' said the prettiest hen, and she laid an egg at Tim's feet.

How joyfully Tim ran home with the answer to the riddle! How gleefully he put the egg on the table!

'Well, have you guessed it?' asked Mrs Rabbit.

'It's there! An egg,' nodded Tim, and they all laughed and said. 'Well, I never! Well, I never thought of that!'

And the prize from Old Jonathan, when Tim gave the answer? It was a little wooden egg, painted blue, and when Tim opened it, there lay a tiny carved hen with feathers of gold.